ANGEL

Also by James Patterson

For more information about James Patterson's novels, visit
www.jamespatterson.co.uk

Or become a fan on Facebook

James Patterson

ANGEL

A MAXIMUM RIDE THRILLER

Century · London

Published by Century, 2011

2 4 6 8 10 9 7 5 3 1

Copyright © James Patterson, 2011

James Patterson has asserted his right under the Copyright, Designs
and Patents Act 1988 to be identified as the author of this work

First published in Great Britain in 2011 by
Century
Random House, 20 Vauxhall Bridge Road,
London SW1V 2SA

www.randomhouse.co.uk

Addresses for companies within The Random House Group Limited can be found at:
www.randomhouse.co.uk/offices.htm

The Random House Group Limited Reg. No. 954009

A CIP catalogue record for this book
is available from the British Library

Hardback ISBN 9781846054662
Trade paperback ISBN 9781846054679

The Random House Group Limited supports The Forest Stewardship
Council (FSC), the leading international forest certification organisation.
All our titles that are printed on Greenpeace approved FSC certified paper
carry the FSC logo. Our paper procurement policy can be found at:
www.rbooks.co.uk/environment

Mixed Sources
Product group from well-managed
forests and other controlled sources
www.fsc.org Cert no. TT-COC-2139
© 1996 Forest Stewardship Council
FSC

Printed and bound in Great Britain by
Clays Ltd, St Ives Plc

To Christian Tabernilla and Palm Beach Day Academy
and to I.S. Rocco Laurie of Staten Island, New York

Many thanks to Gabrielle Charbonnet,
my conspirator, who flies high and cracks wise.
And to Mary Jordan, for brave assistance
and research at every turn.

To the reader

THE IDEA FOR the Maximum Ride series comes from earlier books of mine called *When the Wind Blows* and *The Lake House,* which also feature a character named Max who escapes from a quite despicable School. Most of the similarities end there. Max and the other kids in the Maximum Ride books are not the same Max and kids featured in those two books. Nor do Frannie and Kit play any part in the series. I hope you enjoy the ride anyway.

BOOK
ONE
THE SKY IS FALLING

1

I KNOW HE'LL come for me. He has to come for me. Fang wouldn't let me die here.

I'd been in the cage for days. I couldn't remember eating. I couldn't remember sleeping. I was disoriented from all the tests and the needles and the acrid disinfectant smell that had permeated my entire childhood...growing up in a lab, as an experiment. And here I was again, disoriented but still capable of a blinding rage.

Fang hadn't come for me. I would have to save myself this time.

"You! Get back!" The lab assistant's wooden billy club smashed against the door of the Great Dane–sized dog crate I was being held in every time I peered out through the front. With each strike, the door's hinges sustained more damage. Right according to plan.

Steeling my nerves, I again carefully pushed my fingers out through the bars of the crate and pressed my face against it. Timing was key: if I didn't pull back fast enough, the gorilla-like lab tech could easily crush my fingers or break my nose.

"I said, *get back!*" he repeated. *Smash!* A split-second after the club hit the weakened hinges, I kicked the door with every ounce of strength I had left.

"Hey!" The lab tech's startled yell was cut short as I shot out of the crate, a rush of seriously ticked-off mutant freak, and launched a roundhouse kick to his head. I spun again, leaping onto a table to assess my adversary.

Already a piercing klaxon was splitting the air. Shouts and pounding footsteps from the hallway added to the chaos.

I grabbed on to a pipe on a low section of the ceiling, swung forward, and slammed my feet into a white-lab-coated chest. The bully sank to his knees, unable to draw breath. This was the perfect time for me to run to the end of the table, jump off, and spread my wings.

That's where the "mutant freak" part comes in.

As hands reached for my bare feet, I shot upward, flying toward a small window high in the wall, then veered off path when a familiar dark shadow suddenly loomed.

Fang!

He was on the roof outside, watching through the window. My right-wing man! I *knew* he'd come. He had my back, like a thousand times before. He would always have my back, and I would always have his. With relief, I readied myself to crash through the glass.

The room below me was now filled with shouting people. *So long, suckers,* I thought, as I aimed and got a flying start. I'd burst through quite a few windows in my fifteen-year life, and I knew it would hurt, but I also knew pain didn't matter. Escaping mattered.

Wham! My right shoulder smashed against the glass, but it didn't break. I bounced off it and dropped hard, like a brick. Time slowed. I heard the pop of a tranquilizer gun and felt a dart pinch my leg as I crashed to the ground.

Above me, Fang watched, expressionless.

In disbelief, I realized that he wasn't here to help me after all; he wasn't going to break through the window to save me. I writhed on the shiny linoleum floor, losing consciousness.

Fang didn't have my back. Not this time.

I felt like I was I falling again. Instinct made me scramble to grab on to something, anything.

My fingers latched on to a small, hard branch. As I gasped for air, my eyes popped open, and I realized I was near the top of a tall pine tree—not in a dog crate, not back at the School. The late-morning sun bathed the Arizona mountains in rosy light. It had been a nightmare. Or, rather, a daymare.

I inhaled deeply, feeling the icy claws of adrenaline still in my veins. Cold sweat tickled my forehead and back as I tried to calm down.

It had just been a bad dream. I was free. I was safe.

Except for the worst part of the dream, the one thing that had made everything else a thousand times worse, the one thing that truly terrified and paralyzed me...

Fang really *was* gone. He *didn't* have my back. Not in the dream, not now, *never again*.

2

I HAD BEEN in Arizona a week. A week of being with my mom and my half sister, Ella. A week of having everyone in my flock of winged kids injury free, all at the same time. We had plenty of food, nice beds, and Gazzy had managed to win almost forty dollars from my mom in poker before she wised up. Even now, the tantalizing aroma of chocolate chip cookies (homemade, from scratch, not slice 'n' bake wannabes) wafted out an open window and drifted up to me, perched here atop a huge Apache pine, some ninety feet off the ground.

Everyone was happy and healthy—except me. I mean, I was *healthy*. No bullet wounds, black eyes, or cracked ribs, for once. But happy? Not in this lifetime, baby.

A mere eight days ago, I'd been about as happy as a

fifteen-year-old girl with wings could be. And then Fang, my best friend, my soul mate, my first love—I mean, my *only* love—*took off* without a word. He left me a freaking note. Might as well have cut off my wings while he was at it.

I mean, *he* decided we'd be better apart, you know? It wasn't a joint decision. Like, if you're gonna make a decision about *me* and *my life* for my own good *without* consulting me, I'd better be dying and unconscious, and you'd better be following carefully written instructions.

Anyway. After I had been lying in a fetal position on my bed for twenty-four hours, Nudge called my mom. *So* embarrassing. I've been *shot* and needed less help than I did now. So the flock I've taken care of since forever—Iggy (also fifteen), Nudge (twelve), Gazzy (nine, also called the Gasman, for unfortunate reasons I won't go into here), and seven-year-old Angel—and I (my name is Maximum Ride, aka Max) had flown out here to Arizona. And now *they* were chillaxing—playing Cranium and baking cookies— and I was up a tree by myself, in too much pain to even cry.

Sorry to dump all this on you. You probably popped open this tome hoping to find some kick-butt battles, some pithy wisecracks, some unlikely but oh-so-possible end-of-the-world scenario, only to find me up a tree, wallowing in self-pity. I'm not good at self-pity. I have not done a lot of it. It's not pretty, I know.

You gotta believe I wouldn't be doing this if I could help it. The truth is, I'm hardly even myself anymore. Who is

Max, if not part of "Max and Fang"? Every once in a while, I glanced down at the beautiful, old-fashioned promise ring that Fang had given me not long ago. I threw it away after Fang left, then pawed frantically through the trash until I found it again. Gazzy, watching me, had said, "Good thing you didn't flush it."

This week should have been one of the best weeks of my life. Instead, I would always remember it as a time of bleakne—

With no warning, a voice came from close behind me. "Boo!"

Oh, thank you, I thought, as I jumped and stifled a scream. *Someone to hit.*

3

I WHIRLED AROUND on my branch, muscles coiled to launch myself at my attacker. That's what I'm good at: Fighting. Evading capture. Outwitting bad guys 'n' gals. I am not good at being heartbroken. But then you already knew that.

And what saw I, upon whirling? The Bane of My Existence, Part *Deux*. (Fang is Part *Un*.) Part *Deux*'s name is Dylan.

Instantly my eyes narrowed and my fists clenched. The hot, dry Arizona wind lifted my hair and rustled the pine needles all around us.

Dylan, on a branch not two feet from mine, gave me a mischievous grin. He'd sneaked up on me, and my hearing is *exceptionally* good. The only other person who could do that was Fa—

"What do you want?" I scowled at him.

"What's the matter?" he asked. "Don't know who you are without him?"

"I'm so *sure!*" My eyes glowered, and faster than he could say "Uh-oh," I shot out a hard side kick and knocked him off his branch. I wouldn't have done that a week ago, but a week ago he'd been sweet and lovesick and not a great flyer. When Fang had left and I still wanted nothing to do with Dylan, Dylan had taken a new tack: toughening up, sharpening his sarcastic edge, and honing his flying skills till they were kick-butt.

Dylan is not part of my flock, no matter what he thinks or what he might tell you. He's another recombinant-DNA life-form, a birdkid somewhat like us, except that he was cloned from some original Dylan person, who died some-how. We, the flock, were created in test tubes from mostly human genetic material. And each of us had a little festive dash of avian DNA stirred in, which explains the wings and other amusing physical attributes.

Dylan caught himself before he went splat, shooting out his fifteen-foot wings like sails, letting them fill with wind. With strong strokes, he rocketed upward, determi-nation on his perfect, male-model face, his dark blond hair glistening, and before I could think "Oh no, he *wouldn't,*" he came at me with everything he had, barreling right into me, knocking me off my branch.

My arms windmilled as I fell back, my wings extend-ing. I was dropping fast, fury building, then suddenly Dylan was below me, grabbing me under my arms.

"Get your hands off m—" I started to say, but in the next second, he pulled me close and *kissed* me—hard.

I gasped and my brain just—froze. I couldn't think or feel a single thing.

He let go of me unexpectedly and swooped off. I forgot to flap my wings, and the ground rushed up to me at nauseating speed.

My obituary would read "Killed by love."

4

IF I ACTUALLY DIED, that is, and if I had such a smarmy obit. Which, *please*. Spare me. I beg you.

I caught myself, of course, my wings thrusting with power. My sneakered feet barely grazed the dusty, red clay ground before I surged upward, deciding that killing Dylan was an appropriate response.

He had flown quickly to about a thousand feet, and I shot up to him like an arrow. As soon as I was near, he said, "Admit it! Your heart is pounding!"

"That was the *free fall*," I yelled, circling him in the sky, trying to find the best angle to take him out.

"Look at you!" he taunted. "Moping in a tree! Feeling all sorry for yourself!" He faced me as we circled each other, our wings rising and falling in unison. "Oh, my boyfriend's

gone," he said in a high, squeaky voice, which was, I promise you, *nothing* like my voice. "Oh, what should I do? Oh, I
can't live without him! *Ohhh!*"

A red bloodlust blurred my vision as I darted in to
punch him. He blocked my arm and pushed me back. No
one *ever* talked to me like that. No one would ever *dare*
throw such drivel at me.

"Shut up!" was the best my adrenaline-lit brain could
come up with on such short notice. "You don't know what
I'm thinking or feeling!"

"Yeah, you're sitting in a tree because you're *fine,*" he
said, his handsome face flushed, his turquoise eyes glitter-
ing. "That's easy to see. I can't believe this is *Maximum
Ride,* destroyer of despots, warrior hottie, leader of the
flock! All you need now to make yourself more pathetic is
a pint of Ben and Jerry's ice cream!"

Okay, I've been called everything from arrogant to
zippy, but no one's ever called me pathetic. Had I really
sunk so low?

"Me, pathetic?" I snapped back. "Look in a mirror
lately, loser? I can't stand you, but every time I look up,
you're making cow eyes at me!" I swung my feet forward
and smashed him in the chest—just as I had done to that
whitecoat in my daymare. He let out an "*Oof*" and couldn't
catch his breath for a moment, falling about twenty feet.

Then he rushed back at me, nothing like the thought-
ful, eager-to-please guy he'd been when we'd first met.
Where was he learning how to fight like this?

He whapped me on my side with a powerful wing, making me spin. I'd actually never been hit by a wing before. It's feathery but packs a surprising punch.

"Oh, you can stand me," Dylan said as I righted myself. "You're just afraid to!"

"You're a delusional freak!" I shrieked, trying to drop down to him so I could kick the side of his head. But he feinted and swung to the left, then he grabbed my ankle and yanked hard. My wings bent up painfully. I went horizontal so I could box his ears. He sucked in a breath and let go of me, then I managed a weak kick to his arm.

I got it now. That's where he was learning to fight: from me!

"Why can't you just get out of here and leave me alone?" I bellowed.

"I can't!" Dylan shouted back, his face twisted with an anger I'd never seen from him.

"You can," I said through gritted teeth. "Just point your wings that way and flap!"

"No, I mean, I really can't!" A look of confusion crossed his too-good-looking face. Suddenly, he lost all bitterness and just hovered in the air near me, his wings working smoothly and steadily. He rubbed one hand across his chin. "I actually can't," he said, calmer now, looking at the ground far below us. "And you know why, Max. Don't make me say it." He sounded vulnerable, frustrated.

I'd been told that he had been created—literally created—just *for me*, as my "perfect other half." Let me tell you—if Dylan was my perfect other half, then I needed to give my first half a serious look-see. It all just seemed like total sciencey bullcrap right now.

"I know *why*, Dylan. It's because I'm the only available teenage winged female you've ever met. You might want to wait until they start mass-producing them. Better selection. They've still gotta work all the bugs out." I frowned, thinking of Fang finding a bug-free Max.

"Never, Max," Dylan said. "I'm programmed to imprint on you. You know it. I can't fight the urge to be with you, no matter what."

"That's why you've been stuck to me like glue?" I said. "Because you have to?!"

Dylan frowned at me. "Yeah. I think."

"You think?"

Suddenly his gaze was piercing, haunted. "I think I'd want to be with you even if I were programmed to do the exact opposite."

There was nothing I could say to that. Instead, I folded back my wings and dropped fast to the ground.

5

AH, THE GOOD OLD DAYS, when we were running for our lives, eating out of Dumpsters, getting into life-and-death battles on a regular basis, unable to trust anyone...

That was before I'd found my mom, the woman who had supplied my second X chromosome. I don't usually live with her. I'll always be part of the flock first, and Valencia Martinez's daughter second. Amazingly, she understands that. I love the fact that she exists and cares about me. But as I stepped into her house, I felt a burst of nostalgia for the days when life was hard and dirty and dangerous.

"Taste," Nudge said, shoving a still-warm cookie at me.

My stomach was churning from my little aerial battle with the Cloned Heartthrob, and I wanted to say no.

But she stuck the cookie into my mouth, then peered at

me anxiously as I tried not to gag. "Your mom's teaching me how to cook. Too dry? Too chocolaty?"

"Too chocolaty is an oxymoron," Iggy said from the couch, where he was sitting next to my half sister, Ella. "Okay, go on. You were just at the part where Tarzan kills the big ape."

Ella grinned at me, then found her place on the page and continued reading to Iggy. (He's blind. Lab accident.) As amazing as it was for me to have a real mom, it was equally amazing for me to have a real half sister. I'd been sharing her room at night for the past week, and the conversations we'd had in the dark, when everyone else was asleep, made me feel like a normal teenage girl. That is, until she started talking to me about her crush on Iggy. Then I felt like I was listening to her talking about my son. Who's the same age I am...

Normal's pretty fleeting around here. But right now, across the room, Gazzy and Angel were doing something totally unevil, working a jigsaw puzzle together, and they smiled at me with similar smiles. Of the five (formerly six) of us, they're the only real blood siblings. Which I suppose explains why I have brown hair and brown eyes, Fang has dark hair and darker eyes, Iggy is tall and fair and light-haired, Gazzy and Angel are both blond and deceptively angelic-looking, and Nudge is African American, with light brown skin, curly corkscrew hair almost the same color, and eyes like melted chocolate.

I sighed as I took in the cozy, tranquil domestic scene.

"Hi, honey," my mom said. She came over and pushed my hair behind my shoulders. I tried to remember the last time I'd untangled it, but after I thought back two days, I gave up.

"Hi," I said.

"Why don't you go take a nice shower?" she suggested.

"Yeah, I guess," I said.

Across the room, Angel suddenly cocked her head in a way that made me stiffen and brace myself.

"Someone's coming," she said.

"Who is it?" my mom asked.

Angel concentrated, her brows furrowed. "It's Jeb," she said. "Jeb and Dr. Hans. Hans Gunther-Hagen." And how would she know this, you might ask? Her scary mental powers. She can pick up on people's energy and emotions, from a distance. And close up? Let's just say don't have any private, personal, embarrassing thoughts around her. Yeah. Good luck with that.

"How did they—" I began, then looked at my mom. "You told them we were here?! You know I hate seeing Jeb! And the last time I saw Dr. Hans, he'd just accidentally almost sort of killed Fang!"

"I know, honey," my mom said, looking unruffled. "But Jeb called, and he said he just had to talk to you. Something urgent—he was very insistent."

I looked into her warm brown eyes that were similar to mine. Her hair was darker and curlier than mine. We didn't look much alike.

"I'm not talking to him," I said, starting down the hall to the bathroom.

"If Max doesn't want him here, he shouldn't be here," Dylan said. I looked back to see him swing in gracefully through a large open window. I hated that he was sticking up for me. I'd rather just dislike and mistrust him and be done with it.

"Don't worry, Max," Angel said. She came over to me and took my hand. "Whatever he says, we're in this together. We're the flock."

I stifled a heavy sigh. This from one who was alternately a superamazing, then a traitorous, duplicitous, backstabbing seven-year-old. I didn't exactly trust her fully either.

I looked around. As flock leader, everyone was expecting me to make a decision. Jeb's presence here would bring uncertainty, chaos, probably danger.

It would perk up my day.

I shrugged. "Let him in."

6

WE ALL HEARD IT: the drone of a small airplane. It landed in a dry flat field behind my mom's small house. Gazzy, always hoping for an explosion, seemed disappointed it didn't crash into the trees or go over the nearby cliff.

A minute later, Jeb was at the door with Dr. Hans, who, the last time I'd checked, was still on our official archenemy list. (Yes, we have to keep a list. It's kind of sad.)

My stomach clenched as soon as they walked in the door. Jeb and Dr. Hans together? It was wrong on so many levels. This was the same Jeb who had abandoned us as little kids, forcing us to fend for ourselves in the mountains of Colorado. Ever since then, my relationship with him had been tentative. Tentative like the relationship between a spider and a fly. I am the fly in that scenario.

I looked at Dr. Hans warily, and he looked back at me. He'd almost killed Fang—I'd had to jab a hypodermic needle full of adrenaline directly into Fang's heart to save him. Which, now that I thought about it, was so gross.

Both of these guys could be brilliant, generous, pretty useful, and committed to saving humanity. *Or,* they could embrace the dark side, try to take over the world, or worse: try to make me do something I didn't want to do.

"So much for my vacation," I said, crossing my arms over my chest. To my surprise, Angel copied me, and then so did the rest of the flock. And Dylan. Angel and I have butted heads on more than one occasion, but I have to admit, she'd been pretty sweet to me since Fang had left. This visible show of support nearly brought tears to my eyes.

Oh, my God. I *was* pathetic! Dylan was right.

"It was really more of a staycation," Gazzy mused.

"I'm sorry to interrupt," Jeb said, "but we really need to talk to you, all of you, but especially Max."

"This oughta be good," I said. "Let me guess. We're needed for a research mission at the coldest place on earth?"

"No," said Jeb. "This is bigger than you, bigger than all of us. I need you to open your mind and listen."

"Last time I opened my mind, you injected hallucinations into it," I pointed out. I hardly ever forgive, and I never forget. "Is it…a crazed megalomaniac who has a secret underwater lair where pollution is creating huge, mutant sea monsters?"

"No," said Jeb, looking irritated.

"Yeah, because how likely is that?" I scoffed. "That would never happen! It's crazy!"

"Just hear me out. An evolutionary revolution is happening all over the world."

"Which means what exactly?" I asked.

"Worldwide, a new generation of children with supernatural powers has appeared," Dr. Hans said.

"So far, you're not riveting my attention," I said.

"You know that there are labs and schools all over the world that are trying to speed up the human evolutionary process," Jeb said.

"I do now," I said.

"Dedicated men and women of science are trying to find a way to save the human race. And they've been successful. Overwhelmingly successful, for the first time."

I got a prickle on the back of my neck. The flock and I had been created in just such a lab, a nightmarish place called the School, where another way to say "dedicated men and women of science" was "power-hungry mad scientists with Frankenstein complexes."

"You know that, historically, you've been among the most successful of the recombinant-DNA life-forms," Jeb said. "You were the fifty-fourth generation of DNA experiments."

Some kids get called "bundles of joy" or "slices of heaven" or "dreams come true." We got "the fifty-fourth generation of DNA experiments." Doesn't have the same warm and fuzzy feel. But maybe I'm oversensitive.

"The Erasers were the seventeenth," Jeb said, and we all flinched involuntarily. (If you want to delve more deeply into the wild 'n' wacky world of human-wolf hybrids, check out the earlier Max chronicles.)

"Not that I'm not enjoying this little jaunt down memory lane," I said curtly, "but you're not making a lot of headway here. In fact, so far you're just annoying the heck out of me and making me remember all the reasons I never want to talk to you again."

Jeb glanced at Dr. Hans and then at my mom. She made a face that said, "Way to go, bucko," and he cleared his throat.

"My point is that you guys were successful," he said. "I'm sure you remember all the versions that weren't successful."

"I'll have their catastrophic images burned into my brain till I die," I said. "Are we done here?"

"No," said Dr. Hans. "These children, this new generation, are the ones you'll be leading, after you save the world. It's time you start leading them. Now."

7

OKAY, SLIGHT FLICKER of interest. I'd been doing the "save the world" dance for a while, and so far it had been mostly saving the world one small part at a time. It was exhausting. This sounded more like "big picture" stuff.

"What are you talking about?" My mom's question broke the silence.

"There's like a ton of new mutants?" Nudge asked, her eyes wide.

"We don't use the word 'mutant' anymore," Dr. Hans corrected.

"This new generation," Jeb said, "and it includes children who were genetically engineered as well as a large groundswell of spontaneous genetic evolutions—"

"Or mutations," I butted in.

"We call them Gen 77 kids," he continued. "They're the seventy-seventh generation of genetically modified or genetically enhanced humans. And yes, there are lots of them. Dr. Gunther-Hagen is correct when he says it's time for you to take on your mantle of responsibility, Max. It's very likely that there will be a significant number of these Gen 77 kids among the human survivors of the apocalypse."

"You know, most kids spend their Saturdays arguing about what cartoons to watch," I said. "They don't have the apocalypse thrown at them so early in the day."

"You're not just any kid, Max," Jeb said. "You know that."

"What is this new generation of kids like?" my mom asked. She's a woman of science herself—a veterinarian. Yes, I know. How ironic. Ha-ha.

"They're completely unpredictable," the Hanselator said. "Some of them can breathe underwater, fly, or are telepathic or telekinetic."

(Check, check, check. Not all of us, but Angel is telepathic, and Nudge has been known to draw metal to herself without touching it.)

"Some of them are brilliant," said Dr. H. "Some of them have heatproof skin and can see the thermal images of living creatures."

(Okay, well, whatever.)

"But the important thing is that there are so many of them," said Jeb.

"You are an exceptional leader, Max," Dr. Hans added. "We've been monitoring the astonishing development of this new generation for a while now, and it's imperative that we unite all the Gen 77 kids under one leader—you. Together, we'll be able to prepare them for whatever the future holds."

"Thus far, you've done very well," said Jeb. "But this is only the beginning of your journey. There is much to do to ensure that humans survive."

"Humans in any form?" Dylan spoke up for the first time. "Some people will say that mutants don't deserve to survive at all, much less be among the only survivors."

"We don't use the term 'mutant' anymore," Jeb reminded him. "And yes, there will be detractors, of course. There always are. Which is why Max needs to become their leader now, to start laying the foundation for the New World. With this sudden emergence of enhanced children, we have more weight, more power."

"And that's not all, Max," said Dr. HGH. He'd been looking more and more anxious as our meeting went on, and now he turned toward me eagerly. "There are some crucial developments—"

"Hans!" Jeb said under his breath, "I told you she's not ready for that."

"Not ready for what?" I asked, just as Angel's eyes got big and she slipped off the arm of the couch where she'd been perched.

She put both hands to her cheeks and said, "Oh, no. Not *that!* You have to be kidding!"

I mentioned the whole reading minds thing already, didn't I? It sounded like she'd read Jeb's.

8

"NOT THAT, WHAT?" I demanded, hands on my hips. Jeb and Dr. Hans were looking at each other guiltily, as if they were sending each other telepathic messages. I guess they could have been, but Angel would have ratted them out by now.

"Just tell her," Angel advised, sitting back down.

"We don't have to discuss it now," Jeb finally said unconvincingly.

"Time is running out," Dr. Gub-Hub said.

"She's fourteen!" Jeb countered.

"Fifteen," I reminded him. Everyone in the flock had had a birthday not that long ago. We'd all gotten a year older at once, like racehorses.

"That's still way too young!" Jeb snapped.

"Too young for what?" I was practically shrieking now.

Dr. Hans turned to face me. "Max, you know that we think something catastrophic will happen to our planet, and soon," he said. "And that only some people will survive. And that you will lead the survivors."

"Yeah, I've heard all that," I said. "So?"

"Well, what happens then?" The doctor looked at me intently.

I looked back at him. "We all live happily ever after?"

"No. Say you're the leader. We don't know how long your life span will be..."

Ouch. Call a spade a spade, why don't you? Many recombinant life-forms have built-in expiration dates, when they just suddenly die. The flock and I assumed that we did too.

"Yeah, so?"

"So what happens after you die? Chaos? War? A struggle for power?"

Who the heck even thought that far ahead? I sure didn't. I was still kind of stuck on the whole "save the world" thing at the top of my to-do list.

"Maybe an election?" I offered.

"Elections work in stable societies," Dr. Hans said. "History has shown that emerging societies function better if there is a consistent ruling hierarchy. That's why kings and queens played such prominent roles historically. Only very recently have some countries been able to elect leaders, and even so it hasn't always been successful."

"So what are you saying?" I demanded. "I'm going to be queen?" I tried hard not to picture myself wearing a tiara. It just wouldn't work with the shabby jeans and hoodie look.

"Yes," the doctor said. "In a manner of speaking. And we intend for you to found a dynasty. And that dynasty will rule society until it has progressed enough to—"

"Overthrow the dynasty in a revolutionary, blood-filled coup!" Iggy said eagerly.

We all looked at him.

"Just saying." He sheepishly took a bite of cookie.

"Okay, you lost me," my mom said. "What exactly are you getting at?"

"It's very simple, Dr. Martinez," said Hansey. "We want Max to...breed. To produce heirs. Who will govern the world after she dies."

Dead silence for quite some time. We all stared at Dr. Hans, our jaws dropped to various levels. Our lives had reached a new low of inhumanity.

My face flushed. Part of me had assumed, hoped, that if Fang and I lived long enough, we would get married. Maybe have a little flock of our own. But I really hadn't planned it all out. And he was gone now, anyway. How could I possibly ever find someone...

My eyes scanned Dylan's face. I saw his discomfort.

"Oh, no," I said in horror.

"Yes," Angel confirmed. "Freaking unbelievable."

"It makes sense, Max," Dr. Hans continued as my mind spun. "You two were literally made for each other. You're a perfect match. I'd like you and Dylan to come with me to Germany, where I have a nice home waiting for you. You can marry or not, as you wish, and in time produce children, heirs to your dynasty. To carry on your legacy, your leadership."

"You have *got* to be kidding." My mom's voice was loud. "Over my dead body, Hans."

"Oh, thank you," I said, relieved. "So it's not just me."

"That's a crazy plan!" my mom said. She came over to me and put her arm around my shoulders. "Max is barely fifteen years old! It's bad enough that you've saddled her with saving the world. Now you want her to do it with a baby on her hip? Are you insane?"

I love my mom.

"I'm not saying today or tomorrow," Dr. Gunther-Hagen insisted. "But soon. We're convinced it's the only chance for the world's continued survival."

"Out of the question!" my mom said. "Jeb, this is crazy! How could you?! You're going to drop this right now, or you'll have to leave! I don't want to hear another word about Max breeding with anyone!"

Dr. Hans looked like he wanted to say something else, but he stopped himself.

The worst part? When I cast a surreptitious glance at Dylan and saw the discomfort in his beautiful turquoise eyes morph into a flicker of hope.

9

HE WAS COMING. Fang's first target.

Fang pressed his back against the brick wall, sinking deep into the shadows. For hours he'd been waiting for the gang to disperse, for his guy to head off alone. The group had been shooting hoops, playing dice, smoking and drinking. Fang had heard bottles break and angry disputes dissolve into laughter.

It was late, a bit past midnight. The air was cold. Fang crouched against the wall of the abandoned building, its windows broken and burned out. The deserted lot was full of stuff people probably didn't know how to get rid of: a stripped car, its side still blotched with red Bondo; an old mattress; naked box springs; half a baby's crib, smashed and spray painted.

Fang had been waiting here, still and silent, for most of the night. This was what he'd left the flock to do. This is what Max would not have understood.

He could hear footsteps approaching him. It was his guy, no doubt. An empty glass bottle struck the wall and shattered with a force that seemed unnaturally loud.

Three, two, one...

With precise timing, Fang sprang out from the darkness.

But there was no one there. What the?

Before Fang knew what was happening, the guy had shoved him against the wall, a knife at his throat.

"No one sneaks up on me, *friend*," the hooded figure whispered into Fang's ear. "Been looking for you" — his eyes flashed as he leaned in closer — "and from what I hear, you've been looking for me too."

Fang always kept cool, but he couldn't help letting a smile come to his lips. This guy was good. He was quick and strong and scary. Fang was going to need someone with those qualities on his team. But he wouldn't let himself be subdued so easily, and certainly not by a mere *candidate*. And his first one at that. Fang would be the leader, and he needed to let this guy know who was boss.

With an almost imperceptible flick of his arm, Fang grabbed the hand holding the knife and twisted it behind the guy's back, pinning him. In the same instant Fang's, other hand clapped over the guy's mouth.

"Don't say a word, Ratchet. Your friends can't know I'm here."

Ratchet squinted at Fang in the dark, as if to confirm that this was the same person he'd seen on the blog. Ratchet nodded tentatively, indicating that he was going to cooperate. For now, anyway.

"You make *one* misstep when I let you speak, man," Fang said, "and you lose your teeth." It felt weird to Fang to be threatening another kid, but he couldn't risk being the underdog right now. Fang waited. He had his mission, one he knew he'd been destined for.

Ratchet made a muffled response behind Fang's powerful hand, then Fang released his grip.

"What's the word?" Fang quizzed.

"Maximum," Ratchet said, uttering the password they'd agreed on.

Fang let him go, and Ratchet put on his sunglasses, trying to recoup his swagger. "A'ight, dude. S'long as there're no capes and tights anywhere in your game."

And so it began. This guy made it into Fang's new flock — of one.

10

"NO," I SAID AGAIN.

Just to catch you up, during that brief intermission, all certifiably crazy talk of my producing a feathered dynasty had been dropped, as my mom had insisted. We started eating lunch. But Jeb and Dr. Gunther-Hagen had something else up their dirty sleeves.

"Max, please," Jeb said.

"We're asking you to do this for your own good," said Dr. Über-Goober.

"The stuff you're asking me to do for my own good would stun a yak," I said pointedly. "No."

"My plane is right outside." Jeb tried again. "Or you can fly yourself. I just want you to see the possibilities."

"Nope." I took another bite of PB&J. Even my

mom's peanut-butter sandwiches tasted better than any other peanut-butter sandwiches. I highly recommend having a mom.

"It isn't far—a twenty-minute flight." Jeb tried to sound stern.

"Tough," I said through a mouthful of sandwich.

"Max, this really isn't optional," Dr. Hans said firmly. "The Rocco Laurie School for the Gifted houses many of the children you will be leading when the time comes. They need to be able to recognize you and vice versa."

I gestured at him with my sandwich. "Don't even talk to me." Then I turned to our resident blond cherub. "Angel, what do you think of all of this?" I admit it. I was waiting for Angel to step up and volunteer to be Queen of the World. It was what she'd been wanting. She wanted to run the flock. She wanted to take over my job. She wanted to have power. "Are you interested in meeting this little gaggle of Gen 77 kids?"

But Angel remained uncharacteristically quiet. Calculating her next move maybe.

"You can't just pretend this isn't happening, that you aren't destined for this," Jeb said. I detected a note of frustration in his voice. Good. "The Gen 77 kids need you, whether you acknowledge them or not. Don't you think it makes sense for you to see them? To know them?"

Angel stood up. *Here we go*, I thought. "Max doesn't want to go, Jeb," she said. "So we're not going."

Did she — did she say we're not going? I glanced at her, and she gave me a sweet smile, just like the old days.

"Yeah," said Dylan, coming to stand behind me. "Max leads the flock. If she doesn't want to go, then we don't go."

It would have been churlish to remind Dylan just then that he wasn't part of my flock.

Jeb and Dr. G-H looked like they wanted to tear their hair out.

"Well, you know, I wouldn't mind seeing the Gen 77 kids." I looked up as my mom stepped forward. *Come again?* "Just *see* them." She smiled at me apologetically. "I know how you feel, Max," she went on, noticing the shock twisting my face, "and I don't blame you. But as a scientist, I have an insatiable curiosity. And I think we need to see some of this new generation, whether you lead them or not. We need to know what's going on out there. It's for our own good."

I sighed, beaten. Oh, like I'm gonna tell my mom no?

11

THERE'S SOMETHING ABOUT flying that helps clear the cobwebs from my mind, puts everything into perspective, and makes me feel strong and powerful. And often I can leave annoying people behind on the ground. Always satisfying.

This day, I had left the annoying people in Jeb's airplane, trapped inside a little tin can, while I flew free, chilly air filling my lungs, about two hundred feet away from them. The plane was small, a fancy corporate jet, and everyone—the flock, my mom, Dr. Gub-Hub, the blond DNA donor, and of course Jeb—had opted to travel the easy way.

One odd thing about flying today: the cobwebs weren't

clearing out of my head. Instead, my mind was clouded with misgivings as we flew low over the Arizona mountains. I had not promised to lead the Gen 77 kids. This was a look-see only. I mean, who am I? Joan of Flock? I had my hands full with my own family, my own ~~romantic disasters~~ complications. I couldn't help wondering if this had all been a setup—if Jeb and the Hanster had cooked up this plan to get us interested, to get us on their side. I can't help it—it's just my suspicious nature. That, and the fact that they're both lying, manipulative weasels.

Oh, I see something, Angel thought at me. (She's the only one of us who can project thoughts into other minds at will.) *At two o'clock.*

I looked, and when I squinted, I could see buildings with camouflage netting, in shades of tan and green and brown, over them. Which made them almost impossible to detect from the air. Unless you had super birdkid raptor vision.

Yeah, got it, I thought. *Well, let's go down and see what we can find out.* But way deep inside, I was thinking that maybe I would just hang back, be on my guard, not get sucked into a trap.

Then I remembered that Angel could read minds and that I couldn't actually keep some thoughts deeper inside my head than others.

Crap.

I sped up, leaving the plane behind, and concentrated

on the ground, scanning the area a good distance out. I saw no vehicles, no—

I don't know what made me look up at that moment, but I did, and suddenly, not fifty feet in front of my face, was a huge, clear—jellyfish? I was going almost three hundred miles an hour, and I plowed right into that sucker.

12

IT WAS LIKE hitting a squishy balloon. Going as fast as I was, I sank deep into it, as if I'd hit a bouncy castle face-first and vertically. My head was pressed against a thick, smooth film, and for several horrible moments I had the feeling of being smothered, my wings bent painfully back. Then, *boing!* I bounced out of it, arms and legs flailing wildly, my stalled wings causing me to drop quickly before I could catch myself.

What the heck?!

It had literally bounced me back about sixty feet, and from this distance I could see that it was a huge, clear, weird thing. It was practically invisible, and I realized with shock that there were hundreds of these balloon-type things, each one as big as a city bus. They were all tethered to the ground below by hairlike, glistening metal wires.

Cautiously I got a little closer, and then *zzzip!* The tip of one of my wings brushed a wire, which sliced the ends off some of my primary feathers. It didn't hit skin or bone, but it went through my feathers like they were tissue paper.

It seems the glistening was caused by diamond dust. These wires were designed to slice things—

I whirled, waving my arms at the jet, which was approaching fast, hoping Angel would tune in to my thoughts

Angel! Get Jeb to swerve! This place is booby-trapped!

Angel looked out the window at me, then rushed to the cockpit, yelling.

But it was too late—the plane flew right into the sea of wires.

Almost immediately, one of the engines sucked a balloon-type thing into its intake, and *boom!* There was a huge explosion and a fireball twenty feet across. The force threw me back, heat searing my face and wings. I back-pedaled quickly as several other balloons exploded, tossing the jet to and fro.

Then the wires did to the battered, burned plane what they had done to my feathers. They sheared off the jet's metal wings, like a hot knife through butter.

Can a plane fly without wings? Not so much.

13

FEAR GRIPPED MY HEART as the plane lurched forward, a silent, wingless coffin, the engines dropping earthward as the jet began to nosedive.

Angel pressed her scared face to a window, then was flung to the rear of the plane with the others as the fuselage started to spiral, falling faster, now practically vertical. Almost everyone I loved was trapped inside that metal tube of death.

I let myself drop close to the plane and landed on it with a thunk. I grabbed the door handle, bracing my feet against the side of the plane, but of course I couldn't open the door from outside. In the cockpit, it looked like Jeb and Dr. Hans were shouting orders.

They had only seconds. I saw Dylan grabbing one seat

after another, going hand over hand to reach the door below him.

Angel! Listen to me! I yelled inside my head. *If the door opens, everything inside will be sucked out fast. Get the flock out first!*

Inside the plane, Dylan lost his handhold and fell, then I saw a flash of Nudge hanging upside down, her eyes wide with terror.

Tell the others to let themselves be pulled out and away from the plane. Then Iggy and Nudge should try to grab Jeb. Dylan and Gazzy should grab Dr. Hans. You and I will grab my mom. We can do this! I was thankful that Ella was at school.

I heard someone pounding on the door from the inside, and suddenly it popped open and was ripped off by the force. Instantly, blankets, cups, seat cushions, books, anything that wasn't tied down, whooshed out, a streaming mass of objects moving at deadly speed. A seat cushion whapped me in the forehead, snapping my head back, but I hunkered down and stayed close by.

We were maybe three thousand very short feet up, and my heart was in my throat as I saw Nudge, then Angel, then Gazzy and Iggy jump out of the plane. Dylan, making good use of his genetically enhanced strength, braced his body in the doorway to help keep the others from being sucked out violently by the riptide of air.

"Go south!" I shouted. "Three o'clock!"

Okay. Thank God. My flock was out safely and could

land under their own power. But my mom...I saw her approach the doorway, looking terrified. Dylan yelled something, and she nodded, her face white.

"Help!" Nudge shouted. I spun around to see her caught in the whirling slipstream of the plane—Iggy too! The powerful blast of air had shot them toward the diamond-dust razor wire. There were deep gashes in their wings. Blood spiraled away from them in fine arcs.

"Get out of there!" I yelled, as if that hadn't already occurred to them. Nudge and Iggy were now totally out of control, cartwheeling through the air. The pain in their sliced wings made them want to close them, and the air billowing through their feathers was making their injuries worse. But pulling in their wings meant certain death—they would only drop that much faster.

"Nudge! Iggy!" I screamed as they fell away from me. "Hang on! We'll help you!" Then—

"Max!" my mom shouted and jumped out of the plane. Angel and I shot over to her and grabbed her, synchronizing our wings so they didn't hit each other.

The wind and slipstream tried to pull the three of us away from each other. I concentrated on Angel, seeing the strain on her face. Her wings were powerful; she was using all her strength. My brave little soldier.

Below me, Nudge and Iggy were still struggling, their tattered wings barely keeping them aloft. I made an executive decision.

"Angel, go help Iggy and Nudge," I directed.

Angel looked at me, and I knew that we were both thinking the same thing: Could I hold my mom up by myself? Would Angel even be able to help Iggy and Nudge?

And where were Gazzy, Dylan, Jeb, and Dr. Hans? I couldn't let go of my mom, but everything in me was telling me to save the rest of the flock.

This didn't even qualify as a choice.

14

"SO...YOU IN?" Fang said, meeting the guy's gaze.

Ratchet's face, now hidden behind aviator sunglasses, gave nothing away. In the shadows, his skin seemed to absorb what little light there was. He slouched in the booth, his hoodie pulled up over massive, noise-canceling headphones. Fang had chosen the darkest corner in the diner on purpose, but this guy seemed to think they were still at risk.

Finally, Ratchet nodded. "I'm in, like I told you. But we need to get out of here—fast. My gang won't be happy that I've disappeared. I was, like, their most valuable player, you know? 'The Man' when something was up."

Fang's expression remained neutral. "You were kidnapped," he pointed out. "If anyone saw anything, they'll think it was against your will."

Ratchet shifted uncomfortably in his chair. "It's really loud in here. Think we can go talk somewhere a little quieter?"

Fang glanced at the two other people in the diner—the waitress, who looked to be about sixty, was humming to herself, and a man wearing a trucker hat was sipping coffee alone. Fang raised his eyebrows.

"Wish we could—coffee's terrible—but I'm waiting on another contact. How'd you get messed up in that street business anyway?"

Ratchet let out a breath and shrugged. "My mom. She kicked me out. Thought I was spying on her 'cause I could hear what she was saying anywhere in the house, even when she was whispering. Got to thinking I was a demon or something, reading her thoughts and stuff."

Fang nodded, thinking of Angel.

"Spent a couple of weeks on the street, and let me tell you, it's not as fun as you'd think. I was like a starved rat by the time these brothers picked me up, offering protection. They didn't care if I was a freak, 'cause they needed a lookout."

"How long ago was that?"

Ratchet shrugged. "Four, five months, but when you're in—" Suddenly, he looked up. "Who's she?" Ratchet asked, peering over Fang's shoulder. Fang turned around and looked through the grubby diner window. He saw no one.

"Who?"

Rachet sighed, like it was the most obvious thing in the world. "The blond chick. She's got your name scribbled on a Post-it."

Fang turned around again and squinted. He could just barely make out a figure approaching from two or three blocks away.

He had to admit—he was impressed.

15

FIGHTING PANIC, STAYING ALOFT, Gazzy looked all around him. To his horror, he saw Jeb standing in the doorway of the spiraling, smoking plane.

Another quick look showed no Dylan, no Dr. Hans. Max had Dr. Martinez, and Angel was helping Nudge and Iggy as best she could. That left only Gazzy...

He tucked back his wings, angled his body, and shot down. Gazzy reached Jeb just as he leaped desperately into the air. Moving fast, Gazzy wedged his hands beneath Jeb's flailing arms. Jeb twisted around and clutched Gazzy's forearms, but he hung like dead weight.

"Spread your arms and legs out wide!" Gazzy yelled to Jeb. "It'll help slow you down!"

"I'm too heavy!" Jeb cried into Gazzy's ear. "You can't support my weight by yourself!"

"Uhh," Gazzy said nervously, but it was the truth.

"Gazzy! Listen to me! You all need to know"—he felt Jeb loosen his hold—"the human race will have to die to save the planet!"

Gazzy grimaced and his heart pounded with panic as he watched the ground rushing up at them horribly fast.

"Just like I have to die—to save you!"

And before Gazzy could say anything, Jeb had let go. Reflexively, Gazzy reached out to grab Jeb, even as he dropped ten, twenty, thirty feet away from him in seconds.

"I'm sorry, Jeb!" Gazzy yelled. "I'm sorry!" All he saw was Jeb's face, white and scared, as it got smaller and smaller below him.

Then Gazzy realized that was the last time he would see Jeb alive, ever again.

And it was his fault.

16

STAR LOOKED DISGUSTED by the sushi. And by every-thing else. Her cold blue eyes were dancing between Fang and Ratchet, and Fang wondered if she was about to bolt, to blow this whole thing off. She'd almost wrecked the joint when she learned they didn't serve burgers and shakes.

Ratchet eyed Star's school uniform, her designer bag, and her immaculately painted nails, and scowled. "We don't have very much in common, Twinkle," he huffed. "But sushi's a barfathon, I'll give you that."

"How can you *not like* sushi?" Fang said, spearing another California roll and trying to be sociable to ease the tension. "Wasabi. It's like a party in my mouth."

Star regarded the two of them coolly, her light blond

hair swinging softly around her shoulders. "You guys don't get it. It's not that I don't like it. It just isn't enough. I need more. Bigger. Better."

"Ooh, daddy's little girl is used to *bigger*," Ratchet said in a high, mocking voice. Then returning to a coarse rumble, he said, "I guess size matters to you, huh?"

Star's glare was so icy that Fang almost felt a chill in the air. If it was possible for a Catholic schoolgirl to look lethal, at that moment Star certainly did.

She turned to Fang and said, "I can't work with him."

Then she picked up her chopsticks and began shoveling pieces of sushi into her mouth like a bulldozer. Fang gaped, letting some sushi fall from his chopsticks. This girl was rail thin, and she was putting away more than he and Max could eat—combined. And that was really saying something.

"Will there be anyone else?" Star said, slapping down her chopsticks. She'd managed to eat half the menu in thirty seconds without getting a single drop of sauce on her crisp white blouse.

"Yes," Fang said. "At the hotel. And you also mentioned you had a friend?"

Star nodded. "Kate. She goes to my school. She won't be here for a while yet. She's strong, but I'm fast."

"Guess so," Fang said. "You got here way sooner than I expected. Weren't you coming down here from almost twenty miles north?"

Star shrugged. "I ran."

"In those shoes?" Ratchet snorted. "That's likely."

Fang had to wonder. After all, a twenty-mile run would've had to result in at least a minor sweat, if not a few stray hairs. But Star looked yearbook-photo ready.

"Show us, Star," Fang said with a faint smile of curiosity.

And that was how they ended up "drag racing" until the wee morning hours. Except that it was Fang's wings against Star's feet against Ratchet in a hot-wired Camaro. Star got so bored with winning after a dozen races that she started to give the guys a head start. The more they lost, the more they wanted to win, until Ratchet couldn't stand the embarrassment anymore.

"I give up," he yelled, climbing out of the car and slamming the door extra hard.

"Me too," Fang said, out of breath as he landed, wiping a bead of sweat from his brow.

"So did I pass my audition?" Star asked, with no bead of sweat on her brow to wipe.

"Just barely," Fang grinned. "Okay, folks. Let's get this girl another boatload of sushi. She must be starving."

17

WHEN THE FUSELAGE hit the ground and exploded, I saw my future right below me, just seconds away. My wings were burning, as I gulped air, my muscles shaking from the strain of keeping us both aloft. We were going to land hard—and soon.

"Max!" my mom cried, looking down in horror. For her, Jeb was almost out of sight, dropping to earth like an unaerodynamic rock. Unfortunately for me, because of my raptor vision, I could still make out his terrified expression with utter clarity.

"Gazzy couldn't hold—" I started to say, but then something big dropped past me, actually brushing my feathers and bumping my feet. It was Dylan shooting down to Jeb.

"Go!" I shouted to Gazzy. "Help Angel!"

Gazzy angled his body in a tight arc that brought him close to the others with just a few strokes. He braced himself under Nudge, taking half her weight—possibly reducing her speed enough to keep her from imploding when she hit the ground. Angel focused on guiding Iggy down for what she hoped would be a less-than-fatal landing.

"When we get there, land on your feet, then fall sideways," I told my mom.

Ordinarily, I do a running landing. I can also do a hover-type landing, which involves dropping down from the sky into a standing position. (Kids, don't try that at home—you'll pop your knees.) This time, I rolled sideways, way too close to the ground for comfort, to let my mom slide off me. She landed much harder than I expected and then didn't move. Meanwhile, I tripped and plunged headlong, somersaulting a couple times and coming to a stop on my hands and knees like an amateur.

Right behind me, Dylan and Jeb did about the same. They were still alive, which was all we could really hope for at this point.

About twenty yards away, the ungainly mass of Nudge, Iggy, Angel, and Gazzy finally landed hard, sliding through the red Arizona dirt, then tumbling head over heels, ingesting mouthfuls of sand. Considering that I'd been sure Gazzy would end up being a big Rorschach blot on the ground, I thought they did real well.

I crawled over to my mom. "Mom? Are you okay?"

Gingerly she rolled over onto her back, shading her

eyes from the blazing Arizona sun. "Well, actually, I think my arm's broken," she said. My eyes flew to the arm pinned beneath her. It was bent at an unnatural, nauseating angle. I gently reached for her other hand, her face ashen, her mouth tight with pain.

"And my leg," Jeb said, grimacing.

"Nudge?" I said. "Iggy?"

"Bleeding," Iggy said faintly. "Don't think I can move my wings anymore."

"Me neither," said Nudge, sounding like she was trying not to cry.

"I'm fine," Dylan offered. Then I caught sight of the other side of his face. It was caked with dust and pebbles, blood still oozing, and his lip was split.

"Okay. We need help," I admitted.

Not something you'll hear from me every day.

18

WE'RE NOT FANS of regular hospitals. "We can patch everyone up at my office, do x-rays, put on casts," my mom said. That way, we didn't have to worry about explaining the whole wing situation or the fact that we have bird-type blood — *ix-nay* on any *anfusions-tray*.

I unclipped my cell phone from my belt and handed it to her so she could place a rescue call to her colleagues.

Nudge and Iggy were still bleeding as we waited for help from my mom's office to arrive. I pushed Nudge's hair back from her dusty, scraped face, still shaky from how close to the end we had all come. Gazzy was exhausted, with pulled muscles and banged-up hands and knees. My chest and back muscles ached, and that sliced tip of my wing was sore — but just a little bit. I'd gotten off easy.

"So...no one saw what happened to the good doctor?" I asked.

Everyone shook their heads no. I turned to Dylan.

"And where were you, newbie? Why didn't you jump out of the plane right after Jeb? Was Dr. Hans still in the plane when you jumped?"

Dylan grimaced and nodded. He walked stiffly as if in pain, but everything seemed to be functioning. His face and lip were already scabbing up, since he'd been engineered with the ability to heal himself. "The plane spiraled back and headed into the wires again. If I'd jumped out, I'd have been sliced into deli strips. I yelled at Dr. Hans to jump, but he pushed me out first. Last I knew, he was right behind me, but then he never jumped. I banged my face on the way out."

"Klutz." I snickered, then felt a tiny bit guilty. Dylan had helped everyone else out of the doomed plane, at his own peril. I had to give him props, but how annoying of him to be a hero when I was trying so hard to dislike him. It was downright selfish.

"I want to make sure you don't have a concussion, Dylan," my mom said wanly.

Dylan shook his head. "Sorry—I'm not going back with you. I've gotta find what's left of Hans and the plane. Thought I would do some recon after you guys head off."

"I'd feel better if you had an x-ray," my mom protested.

"Later," Dylan promised. "There's no way I can let this go. I have to find Hans, if only so we can send his body back to Germany."

I understood where he was coming from. There were so many ifs, buts, and maybes in our topsy-turvy world, it was comforting to nail down as many details as possible. Even if that meant finding his unquestionably evil creator in pieces.

"Max, you'll come with us, won't you?" my mom said, her face drawn with pain.

I wanted to say, "Yeah, of course," but the words got stuck in my throat. I paused for a moment, thinking, then had a stunning realization—and this is just between you, me, and this cactus here. I didn't want to let Dylan go off on his own.

And it wasn't even for a good reason, like I didn't trust him and wanted to make sure he wasn't in league with Hans.

It was just that I didn't want to leave him. Something in me wanted to stay with him.

I had two follow-up thoughts: *Why???* And *Ew!!!*

Dylan had said that he'd been programmed to want to be with me. Was it possible that I'd somehow been programmed for him? Nah, there was no way, not after what Fang and I had meant to each other.

My face must have shown my confusion, because my mom said, "What is it? Are you hurt?"

"I think I'll go with . . . Dylan," I heard myself say. I felt like a traitor, leaving my injured flock. But they had my mom—and even Jeb, as long as he didn't turn into a back-stabbing weasel.

When I looked at Dylan, I saw surprise on his face and then a rush of pleasure, and I felt . . . good.

19

"WE'LL BE OKAY," Angel said to me, as my mom's office manager climbed back into the front seat of the van. "You do what you need to do." I got the embarrassing feeling that Angel wasn't just talking about finding Hansy. Then my injured flock was driving across the bare land, and it was Dylan and me, alone, as the trail of dust kicked up by their departure gradually settled and the van disappeared from view.

Now that we were alone, I was self-conscious and cranky again. Why had I wanted to stay? If I had been programmed to want to be with Dylan and only Dylan, heads were gonna roll, I promise you that.

"So," Dylan said calmly. "I'm thinking the plane probably

went down a mile or so to the southwest of here. At least, that was the direction it was heading when I left it."

"That makes sense." I nodded, relieved he wasn't trying to convince me to run off with him to find a cozy little nest for two.

"So let's do this thing," he said, and made a running takeoff that was beautiful to see. I taught him how to do that only weeks ago. It was amazing how far his skills had advanced since then. Taller and more sturdily built than Fang, Dylan soared powerfully into the sky. The sunlight glinted off his hair, and his feathers shimmered. His wings were a little shorter than Fang's but broader—more like a hawk's—wings built for power and lift. The rest of us had wings that were narrower and more angled, designed for speed. For the first time, it occurred to me that the mad scientists who created us might have used different avian DNA to make each of us.

I had never thought of that before. I had sort of assumed that they'd had one vial of avian DNA and had gone around with an eyedropper, plopping it into our test tubes. The idea that they might have paired us with birds having different characteristics amazed me. So far, none of us seemed to have flamingo as part of our makeup, or penguin. There's always something to be thankful for.

"Are you coming or what?" Dylan shouted to me. He'd been circling, waiting for me while I took a quick ride on my train of thought.

I started running, building speed, and after about thirty

feet I threw myself into the air and whipped out my wings. I pushed down with hard, even strokes, rising fast. The sun shone on my face, my tangled hair streamed behind me, and I felt a burst of pride at my strength and the sheer joy of flying.

Dylan seemed to know what I was thinking. He grinned at me, even with his bruised face and swollen, blood-caked lip, and said, "There's really nothing better."

I nodded, then thought a moment. And here's the weird part: at the exact same time, Dylan and I both said, "Except a white-chocolate mocha from Coffee Madness."

We stared at each other as our voices trailed off. This wasn't a "jinx" kind of thing, when we both said "yep" at the same time or anything like that. It was a long, weird sentence, and we had said it simultaneously.

Can you read my mind? I thought, but if he could, he was smart enough not to tell me. Instead, he frowned.

"Can you read my mind?" he asked accusingly.

Also a smart move. Offense is a strong defense.

"No!" I blurted, glaring at him.

It was weird. It was scary. And yet... I didn't leave.

20

"HELLOOO, KATE!" RATCHET said, then whistled. "I think my senses just short-circuited."

Fang cringed. Well, this was going to be fun. He had wanted mostly older kids so he wouldn't have to worry about them, and now he had to deal with freaking flirting instead.

Kate Tan Wei Ying had finally arrived on the scene, and the girl was a bombshell. She had thick, glossy black hair that wouldn't stay tucked behind her ears, supermodel cheekbones, and an easy smile. And she had her own cause, it turned out.

"You're what?" Ratchet looked horrified.

Kate laughed and pushed her hair off her shoulder. "I'm

vegan," she repeated. "I don't eat meat, seafood, or anything that comes from animals, like milk or butter or eggs."

Ratchet looked at Fang like, *First freaking sushi, now this?* Fang shrugged. "I'm glad I booked us into nice digs." He plopped down on one of the beds and started flicking through the channels. "I hear the hotel grub is pretty sweet."

"You guys can still get room service," Kate said good-naturedly. "I brought Tofurky Jerky to snack on."

She was the opposite of razor-tongued Star, and given the look Star was shooting her, it was a little weird that they were friends. But then, maybe freaks just tended to find each other. And Kate and Star were certainly freaks. Ratchet was one thing—the tough street kid who had extrasensory skills. The girls were...something else.

Fang sighed. He should've just gone with guys. Way less complicated. He tried to focus on the news and not think about the fact that she would be here soon.

"And now back to Channel Seven News on the Hour," said an announcer, and then two talking heads filled the TV screen. "A new environmental group is garnering attention worldwide." A concerned woman with perfectly coiffed hair leaned forward slightly. "But what does their name mean, Dan? The Doomsday Group?"

Fang sat bolt upright. He turned up the volume, waving the other kids to be quiet.

Dan shook his head gravely. "We have very little information on the group at this time, Sheila. Calls to the organization have not yet been returned. I want to stress that, at present, no allegations have been made against the group, but its name is certainly attracting attention."

Sheila consulted her notes. "Our European correspondent is standing by in Paris, where a Doomsday Group rally took place earlier. Perhaps she can provide us with a keener look into the group's motivations. Sofia?"

The camera cut to a woman standing in front of the Eiffel Tower, her khaki trenchcoat flapping in the wind. "Greetings, Sheila," she said with a French accent. "This is Sofia Tabernilla reporting from Paris, where the so-called Doomsday Group has been very active today."

Behind her, Fang saw smiling people chatting with passersby and handing out leaflets.

"Sofia?" Sheila asked, pressing her fingers to her earpiece. "Can you tell us what the group is distributing?"

Sofia frowned. "Flyers. Notices." Sofia held one up and read from it: "This is the group's slogan, printed here in English, French, German, and Dutch. It says, 'The Earth or Us.'

"I'm here with one of the key organizers of the Doomsday Group rally, though the group professes to have no leader. Beth, can you tell us more about your group's message and your goals as an organization?" Sofia held the microphone out to an older-looking teenage girl.

"Our goal is to bring everyone to the One Light." She had one of the sweetest voices Fang had ever heard, but her eyes were what drew him in. "It's an invitation for change. We plan to take control for the betterment of the earth."

"Take control?" Sofia Tabernilla asked, but she was smiling serenely at her. Beth nodded, smiling back.

"Think of it as an earth cleanse. It will be beautiful. Follow us. Follow us and be free." She looked directly into the camera, and Fang was mesmerized. The group would save him. Beth would save him. She would help him forget all the harsh—

Star clicked the remote, and the theme song for *Project Runway* made Fang jump.

His head was buzzing. He felt happy and calm. He felt like everything was going to be beautiful. He shook his head.

Something was seriously wrong.

A group that had sprung up out of nowhere and already had international coverage? Talking about cleansing the earth and taking control? The Doomsday Group set off every antennae of alarm Fang had.

A quick online search for the Doomsday Group revealed surprisingly little, as if it had sprung up suddenly, fully formed. There was no mention of it at all two months earlier, but clearly its members already numbered in the thousands.

Fang sat back. He had his mission.

Someone had to figure out what the Doomsday Group

was up to and just how bad it was. It was time for Fang to step up and be a leader, the way Max always had.

A familiar ache filled his heart, and he promptly squelched it. No time for that now. He had too much to do. She wasn't the only one with a mission to save the world.

Now it was just a question of who would save it first.

21

"I'M NOT SEEING anything," Dylan said a good twenty minutes later. "I mean, I see the wires. I see where we all hit the ground. The plane's sheared-off wings are over there, all in pieces. I can even see the plane's door that ripped off. But what I don't see is—"

"Hans. Or the plane's fuselage," I interrupted.

"You read my mind again!" said Dylan, and I glared at him.

"No, it's just the obvious huge missing thing. I have a brain. I can think."

"I know that," Dylan said mildly. "I was just teasing."

Now I felt like a clod. I rolled my shoulders to release some tension. "So where do you think it is?" I am highly skilled at changing the subject as demonstrated here.

"It was already smoking and spiraling by the time I got out," he said. "I didn't think it would get far at all."

"We should check under the cloud of balloon-type things," I said, and Dylan nodded as he started a wide, smooth, arcing turn.

"Show me how to fly sideways," he called over his shoulder. "That was cool."

"The hawks taught us that," I said. "Basically, you roll and point one wing down. Then keep flapping. You'll keep moving forward, even though it feels weird."

Dylan tried it. The first couple of times he looked a little clumsy, but when we reached the wires of death, he was flipping sideways like a pro, powerful and smooth. His learning curve was really amazing.

"Man, each tiny wire has four sides, like a four-sided razor," he said as we carefully started flying through the wires.

"You can see that?" I asked.

"Yeah. I can see really far, really close, and sometimes right through stuff." He turned back to grin at me, and I wondered what kind of things he could see right through.

"I guess you're the improved version of me," I said coolly. "I have great vision but not like that. I mean, I can see the school building way down there but not the four sides of the wires."

He smiled at me. "Everyone has strengths and weaknesses," he said with irritating modesty. So far, I had seen only strengths and no weaknesses from him. But I wasn't about to say that.

"I'm not seeing squat, other than the school," I reported. "And we already knew that was there. Let's broaden our search area."

"Good idea," said Dylan, and ten seconds later we were out of those awful wires and in the open blue sky.

I breathed deeply, enjoying the sun on my face. For several minutes we flew in silence, hearing just the sounds of our wings and the occasional bird. After a while of finding no Hans remnants, I said, "Let's check out the school anyway."

Dylan said the exact same thing at the exact same time. Again.

22

"I THOUGHT THIS Doomsday stuff was, like, urgent," Star said. "Who's this girl we're waiting for?" Star was devouring another hot dog from room service, her third, while Kate looked on, repulsed.

"And how come all we're getting is chicks?" Ratchet asked Fang. "Not that I'm complaining." He lifted his sunglasses to peer at Kate.

"Nobody says 'chick' anymore." Kate rolled her eyes.

Ratchet grinned at her, his bright smile lighting his face. "Okay, I hear you." He turned back to Fang. "How come all we're getting is babes?"

"She's just someone I know from a while ago," Fang said in a controlled voice from behind his computer. "And there's another guy on the way too, Ratchet. He's the last one. They both should be here soon. For now, I guess we just chill."

Not five minutes later, Star's angry voice made Fang look up. She was standing over Ratchet, who was sprawled across one of the double beds. "I was watching that! You can't just change the channel!"

"There's a game on," Ratchet said. "You watch your little show in the other room."

"The TV's broken in there," Star snapped. "How can you even see it with those stupid sunglasses on or hear it through those headphones, anyway? Give me the remote."

Ratchet shrugged, looking bored, and turned the volume down even lower.

"Listen, street punk," Star snarled, her angry face close to his. "You're a guy, and you're a couple inches taller, and maybe forty pounds heavier, and ooh, you're in a gang. But I've survived ten years of Catholic school, and I will cut you off at the knees without a blink. Do you understand?" She snatched the remote from his hand and in a millisecond was halfway down the hall.

"Your daddy pay for that attitude?" Ratchet called after her.

Everything happened fast after that. Before Fang could even ask what was going on, Star had zipped back into the room like a bullet, but Ratchet's hypersenses had tipped him off, and he was ready for her. But before either of them could make contact, Kate had both of Star's hands clamped in one of hers and her left knee firmly on Ratchet's chest, pinning him hard to the floor.

"I said I don't like violence," she said quietly. "Maybe you two should cool off."

Ratchet grinned up at her goofily. "Kate the Great." He wheezed. "I think I'm in love."

"Guys, guys," Fang said, raising his voice until they all looked at him. "Kate's right. Maybe you should check your egos. We're all really different. Don't you realize that that's exactly why I picked you, out of everyone who applied on the blog? For example, what might defeat Ratchet might not defeat Star."

Star smirked, and Fang cleared his throat. He hated talking so much — he'd never known that all the talking Max did was necessary, as a leader. He'd been realizing a lot of things about Max lately.

"That means that it'll be tough for us to work together as a group, but you need to suck it up, try to get along, and treat each other with respect. If you don't feel like you can do that, then leave now, no hard feelings." Fang felt their surprise. He looked into each of their faces, but no one stepped forward.

"Fang's gang," Ratchet said from the floor. "Got it, bro." The girls nodded in agreement.

"Okay, then. I guess we're all straight on that," Fang said.

"Straight on what?" Max said from behind him.

Fang's heart almost stopped.

23

FANG SPUN AROUND and saw Max standing there, giving him the sardonic smile he knew so well.

"Straight on the fact that we need to work together as a team," Fang managed to say. His heart contracted painfully inside his chest, then started beating again. "Where'd you come from?"

Max smirked and pointed at the sky, then wriggled a bit, adjusting her wings under her oversized windbreaker. "This was where we were supposed to meet, right?" She scanned the rest of Fang's gang.

"Yeah," Fang said, taking a deep breath. God help him, she even smelled familiar. "It's been a long time."

"Has it?" Max cocked her head and looked him up and down. "It feels like we just saw each other."

Fang sighed. Maybe this hadn't been such a good idea. He'd underestimated how he'd react to her. Way underestimated.

Max flipped her light brown hair over one shoulder, and Fang noticed that she'd dyed a big magenta streak in part of it. Other than that, she looked exactly the same.

Exactly the same as the Max he'd left barely more than a week ago, back in Colorado. He wondered what she was doing now, what she'd think about his joining forces with...her. The other her, that is. Max the Clone. Max II.

"Hi, I'm Kate," Kate said, extending her hand.

Max II looked at the hand, then shook it, a smile lifting one side of her mouth. Max's mouth. The mouth Fang had kissed so many times. Blood was rushing through his head, and he needed to clear it, to take control of this situation again. Worse, he had the feeling that this Max knew exactly what he was thinking, could read his mind, and was somehow laughing at him.

"And this is Star," Kate said, pointing. "And that's... Ratchet."

"Yo." Ratchet had gotten up off the floor, but his hands were buried in the pockets of his hoodie. "Cool hair. Is it dyed in blood or something? 'Cause that would be hard-core."

Max II snickered, unphased by his comment.

"And what's your name?" Star asked politely, but in the twenty-four hours Fang had known her, he'd learned to recognize the tone of warning beneath her politeness.

"Her name is—" Fang began, but Max II interrupted him.

"Maya. They call me Maya." She shoved her hands into her pockets and sat down on one of the beds, daring him to contradict her.

Fang blinked. So she had changed her name. He couldn't blame her.

"You okay, dude?" Rachet elbowed Fang in the ribs. "You're looking a little green around the gills."

Fang nodded his head, avoiding Maya's eyes. "I'm fine. We just—go back a long time."

Ratchet eyed the tips of Maya's wings sticking out of her coat and gave a low whistle. "Say no more, man. I get you. You guys were all Swan Lake, doing the lovebird dance, and now it's a little Emotions on Ice." He looked at Kate. "I go for the Wonder Woman type myself."

Kate's smooth Asian face flushed bright red, and Star looked disgusted. "Maybe he could use another knee to the jugular," she suggested.

Maya laughed. "Fun little group you got here."

Fang forced a smile and nodded. This had been a huge mistake.

BOOK TWO

WHAT'S SO FUNNY 'BOUT PEACE, LOVE, AND WORLD DESTRUCTION?

24

"DO YOU SEE any guards?" I asked Dylan. Of course, I was still quietly freaking out about the second "coincidence," but he didn't need to know that...

"Not yet," he said. "But they must be there. Are we thinking drop down onto the roof? Or land in the desert, then sneak up?"

"Roof," I said, and he nodded. I hated it when he was agreeable.

Naturally, they weren't going to let us just drop down onto the roof. My life could never be that easy. After all, this was a top-secret facility where new life-forms were being created. You think they'd let strangers plunk right down onto the roof?

No.

As soon as we were within three hundred feet, a door on the roof swung open, and figures all in black complete with ninja hoods, leaped out. They popped rifles up on their shoulders and took aim.

"Evasive maneuvers!" I yelled, but Dylan was already matching me zig for zag as we poured on the speed, blazing into the sky.

A bullet whistled past my ear. They were using long-distance sniper's rifles.

"Watch it, Max!" Dylan grabbed my hand and yanked me to the left, just as another bullet streaked by, right where my head had been. I gaped at him, and he dropped my hand sheepishly. He shrugged. "I saw the guy aim."

The people on the roof were little stick figures by now. Another hundred feet up and they'd disappear from my view.

"Freaking whitecoats!" I screamed, even though they'd been dressed in black. "So, what? You think if you can create life, you can destroy it too?"

Dylan looked down again, squinting. "Wait. They're not whitecoats," he said. "They're not even grown-ups. They're . . . I think they're kids."

"Oh, come on," I protested. "They might have been a little short, but—"

"I could see them," Dylan insisted, sounding agitated. "Inside their masks. They were kids, Max. I'm positive. And it gets worse. They didn't, they didn't have—eyes."

"What?" I gasped. We'd reached a good cruising altitude, well out of range of fire. From this height, the land below looked like a crazy quilt stitched together.

"They didn't have eyes," he repeated, genuinely troubled.

"Great, give the blind kids guns," I said, trying to lessen his horror. "I don't even let Iggy have a gun. Usually." I glanced over at Dylan, but he wasn't smiling.

"But…they could still aim. They still knew we were there, somehow," he said.

"They must have some sort of alternate sensing system. I wonder if they have no eyes on purpose, or if it was a mistake? I mean, Iggy is blind because they operated on him, trying to give him better night vision."

Dylan looked appalled. "You're kidding."

"Don't you get it?" I couldn't keep the bitterness out of my voice. "People like that—mad-scientist types—we aren't human to them. We're experiments. And those kids down there, kids who have been trained to kill, kids who have no eyes—they're experiments too."

"That's all we'll ever be, isn't it?" Dylan shook his head sadly. "Lab rats. Just someone's theory, someone's pipe dream. And they've already replaced us with the next best thing."

He looked so pitiful, so lost, that before I even knew what I was doing, I took his hand in mine. On purpose. It was warm and soft. Not battle hardened yet.

Then I said something that I've said very rarely in my life—even more rarely than "I love you."

"I'm sorry," I told him.

25

DYLAN GAVE MY hand a squeeze and smiled weakly. Out of nowhere, I had a vision of kissing those soft, perfect lips. Then Fang's face flashed before my eyes. I fell into a sudden coughing fit and dropped Dylan's hand like a dead fish.

"You okay?" Dylan asked, rubbing my back. When I glared at him, he, thankfully, had the decency to change the subject.

"It's later than I thought," he said. "I say we camp out in the desert tonight, spy on the school from a distance, and maybe find a way to sneak in tomorrow morning."

"Huh," I said. It was a plan that I might have come up with, probably would have come up with. But all I heard, all I focused on were the words, "camp out in the desert tonight." The two of us. Alone. And my heart sped up.

About a mile from the Gen 77 school, there were

canyons, striped with layers of red, peach, and cream-colored rock. We flew toward one of the higher buttes and found a natural cave with an excellent view of the school. Then it was Dylan and me, alone together.

If he tried anything, I'd knock his teeth out.

You're meant to be together, the Voice said suddenly. I groaned so loud that Dylan looked startled.

"It's nothing," I muttered.

"Okayyy," he said quizzically, and I was back to wanting to punch him. "Hungry?" Dylan reached into his pocket and pulled out a couple of protein bars. I took the chocolate chip one. It tasted like sawdust mixed with chocolate chips. I was glad to have it. I contributed a bottle of warm water. We shared it in silence.

"I hope the others aren't too worried," I said, trying to make conversation, my voice sounding weirdly loud in the still night.

"They have to know by now that you can take care of yourself," said Dylan. I nodded in agreement.

For long moments, we lay on the ledge on our stomachs, watching the school. With Fang, silences were comfortable. With Dylan, they were awkward. After a while, Dylan leaned over my shoulder and pointed up.

"Ursa Major. And Pegasus, the winged horse. Kinda looks like us." I followed as his finger traced the shapes. The stars were bright and so numerous that it looked like someone had taken a handful of diamonds and thrown them onto black velvet.

"Or, no, there's you, Max. Cassiopeia, the queen."

"Oh, come on!" I cuffed him on the shoulder, and he tucked his head down, laughing. Still, I felt my face getting warm.

"Where'd you learn all that stuff, anyway?" I asked seriously. He shrugged.

"Back at the house in Colorado. When you were— away." He cleared his throat, and I gulped. He meant when I was away *with Fang*. "The rest of us watched the stars. They said Jeb had taught you guys about them back in the day. Don't you remember?"

Now it was my turn to shrug. I'd blocked out most of my good memories of Jeb.

"I was interested, and I had a lot of time to myself over there. So I read up on it. I'm curious about stuff, I guess. I just sort of absorb information."

I thought of our Max's Home School sessions, about how the rest of the flock had resented me for wanting us to learn something. I kept my eyes focused on the school building below.

"Do you think you could, like, teach me some of that stuff sometime?" I asked, in a small voice that didn't even sound like me. It sounded cheesy.

Dylan didn't laugh. "Of course," he said. I felt his deep turquoise eyes looking right into me. "Anytime you want, Max."

"Thanks," I whispered, then trained my eyes back on the facility. Lights were on in the building, but no vehicles came or went, and no one seemed to step foot outside. I tried not to notice the warmth coming from Dylan's body, or how every once in a while one of his sneakers nudged mine.

"I'm luckier than you are," Dylan said unexpectedly.

"How do you figure that?" I asked, looking at him in the dark.

"I know you're torn up about Fang," he said. I cringed. "I don't blame you. And now I'm here, and everyone's pushing me at you, including me."

My cheeks burned. This was exactly the kind of horrible, embarrassing, emotional stuff that I try really hard to avoid. Maybe if I talked about how to skin a desert rat, it would kill the romantic mood . . .

"But for me, there's only been you," he continued, looking off into the distance. "I don't have to make any decisions. I don't have to figure things out. You're the only choice I have, the only one I want. For me, it's really simple."

I swallowed, feeling like there was a large brick in my suddenly dry throat.

"You don't know me," Dylan said. "You and Fang—you kind of talk the same, figure things out the same, know a lot of the same stuff, have a lot of shared history. You and I are more . . . combustible," he said softly.

I couldn't look at him. I felt as if looking at him would somehow break down every barrier I'd put up between us. I knew without a doubt that I loved Fang. But Dylan had hit the nail on the head—he and I were combustible. If I were mad at Fang, it was more like stubborn opposition, irritation. If I were mad at Dylan, it was fury, white hot.

I'm a girl who has been tamping down her emotions and keeping them tightly guarded her whole life. And that works really well for me. But that approach didn't seem possible with Dylan. He provoked me; he got under my skin. And now I felt like my shell had a dangerous crack in it. Without much more effort on his part, it would split wide open, and my enormous river of emotions would gush out—the bad and the good.

It was pretty much the scariest thing I'd ever thought of.

I rested my head on my arms and closed my eyes, unable to say a word. It had been a long, hard day. I tensed when I felt Dylan's fingers smooth my hair, then slowly trace a line down my back. When I didn't say anything, he lay next to me quietly and put his arm around my shoulders.

He didn't speak again, and gradually my muscles relaxed in his warmth. And I noticed how well my body curved into his...a perfect fit.

As if we were engineered that way.

I fell into a deep sleep tucked in that little cocoon, a deeper sleep than I might have had in years.

Right up until someone kicked me and said, "Gotcha!"

26

I JUMPED TO my feet and landed in a semicrouched position, fists at the ready.

Angel put her hands on her hips and pursed her lips. "Very fierce," she said. "It would have been much fiercer if I hadn't been able to sneak up on you while you were sleeping."

She raised an eyebrow. I resisted looking at Dylan, who was now standing beside me, but I felt my ears get warm as I remembered the way we'd fallen asleep last night, his arm around me.

"Hi," I said inadequately, and pushed my dusty hair out of my eyes.

"Yeah," she said dryly. "Once everyone was back home and patched up, I wanted to come find you, to make sure you were okay."

"I'm always okay," I said. "How's everyone else?"

"Pretty good. Your mom has a cast on her arm. Jeb has a cast on his leg. Iggy and Nudge are actually kind of a mess—Nudge needed eighty-seven stitches, and Iggy got a hundred and three. Gazzy has two cracked ribs."

My eyes widened. I'd left them...

"But they're okay, really," Angel went on. "They'll heal fast. So, what's the deal down there, anyway?" I quickly caught her up on the eyeless kids guarding the school.

She sighed deeply and shook her head. "When will they learn? Poor kids."

"Don't feel too sorry for them. Even without eyes, their aim was still pretty accurate. Hey, can you pick up anything coming from there, thoughtwise?" I asked.

Angel sat very still and closed her eyes. Dylan and I sat down too, but I refused to look at him. After a couple minutes, Angel frowned and opened her eyes.

"I didn't get anything," she said. "You're sure they're humanoid, not bots of some kind?"

Dylan laughed. "Yeah, like robots, covered with skin and stuff? Science fiction."

"You have much to learn, Grasshopper," I said, then turned to Angel. "What say we fly overhead and lure them out. When you see them, you can try to play puppet master and get them to put down their weapons. Sound good?"

Angel nodded, stood up, and brushed off her jeans. "Let's do it."

We had to go through the horrible razor wires to get close to the school. It was nerve-racking, and now I was burdened with the image of Nudge and Iggy being all sliced up and stitched back together again. But, pros that we are, we zipped through the obstacle course and emerged over the school. It took a few minutes before the rooftop door opened, and, surprise, three black-hooded guards raced out, weapons raised.

Angel stared at them, willing them to lower their weapons. Once or twice, we saw a couple of them falter and start to lower their rifles, but then it was like an override feature kicked in, and they straightened up and prepared to fire.

"They've been brainwashed," Angel said slowly. "I can barely get through at all, and then only for a second before their programming takes over."

"Are they human?" I asked.

"Yeah, mostly," she said. "Combined with something, but I don't know what. When I got in one's head for a moment, I saw how it sees. We looked like glowing things in the sky, very bright."

"Hence, their uncanny aim," I said. Then I had a thought. "If we're glowy things in the sky, what happens if they see a falling star?" And with that, I simply closed my wings and dropped down to the roof, extending my wings at the last second to break my fall. The ninja kids paused, hesitating, then quickly raised their weapons, aiming at me point-blank.

I held up my hands in the universal "I'm unarmed and if you shoot me you're a total unfair jerk" gesture, but only heard safeties clicking off in response.

"Plan B!" I yelled, dropping and rolling to the side. In this case, plan B was "fight like crazed wolverines because plan A went nowhere." I swung a leg out, fast and hard, and knocked one attacker's feet right out from under him or her.

Everything got kind of messy after that.

27

ANGEL SHOT UP in the air just as one ninja kid fired at her, but when she landed behind him, the kid's leg flung out and nailed her in the gut. Coughing, she lunged for the rifle, but again the kid anticipated her position and smashed her knuckles.

Angel's pretty quick when she needs to be, but the ninja kid was always one step ahead of her. What was the deal with these creepsters?

I was scrambling to my feet to help Angel when one kid sprung at me, weirdly fast, in a series of backflips. I swerved sideways at the last second, but, with lightning-fast reflexes, the kid snap kicked me right under the chin. I was shocked. My arms windmilled and I fell backward, off the building.

Just as my fingers snagged the edge of the roof, I got a glimpse of Dylan's furious face as he charged the kid who'd kicked me. But I didn't need Prince Charming. I had already bounced back and flown up on the roof—only to be shot at as soon as I was visible.

My head was ringing, my teeth had slammed together, and I tasted blood.

"Okay, enough!" I snapped, really angry now. I still had a roundhouse kick or two in me, and I was ready to start whaling on these bullies. I surged forward while one took aim, but then I spotted Dylan waving his arms at me to stop.

Which, come on, didn't Golden Boy here know me at all?

He was pointing at the sky and mumbling something about how they couldn't see. I glared at him. *Yeah, Dylan, we've established that.*

"Over their heads," he shouted. "I don't think they can sense anything directly over them!"

I looked at Angel, who was hovering over a confused-looking ninja kid. He was spinning around but couldn't seem to get a read on her.

Oh. Got it!

Dylan and I joined Angel in zipping from kid to kid, moving as quickly as possible, so that the ones we weren't directly over couldn't get a good shot. It wasn't long before the kids were spinning in place, trying to focus.

If it hadn't been so screwed up, and we weren't actually, you know, dancing over the heads of kids trying to kill us, it might've been kind of fun. But somehow I didn't think that this strategy was going to end our little skirmish.

Just as I was about to call for a plan C, the ninja kid below me dropped to the ground. And so did the one spinning underneath Dylan. *Say wha...?* They seemed to be short-circuiting or something. After the third one fell, we snapped cord ties around their wrists.

When it was over, I sat back, panting, watching the bodies warily to make sure they stayed down as Dylan double-checked that all guns were accounted for.

Angel leaned over and yanked off one ninja kid's black hood.

It was awful.

He looked just like a regular kid, but he had a small slit above his nose — a slit that ran around the circumference of his head, like a ring. And in that slit, I saw...many eyes. Tiny, dark orbs, angrily zipping back and forth. He wasn't blind at all. He had 360-degree vision. They were virtually impossible to sneak up on, except from above, apparently.

"And I thought *we* were paranoid," Angel said quietly.

"Yeah," I said. "These guys are paranoia incarnate."

Dylan was shocked and silent. I'd thought genetic mistakes were the height of horribleness. I hadn't realized that genetic "successes" like these 'noids might be even worse.

28

"WHO MADE YOU this way?" I whispered, horrified. "And why?"

They were just kids. Kids like us who had been cut open and experimented on, kids who had been programmed to kill us, but still.

The 'noid we'd been looking at wriggled onto his side, his slit of eyes racing. He didn't look older than nine or ten.

"We've been created to have an advantage—over the humans who have mucked up the planet, and over you and all earlier generations of improvements. The world is going to end, and when the time comes, we'll... take over."

I rolled my eyes. Serious brainwashing here.

"Look, Spider Eyes, we know the world isn't in good

shape. That's why we're trying to take steps to fix things. Which would be a whole lot easier if people like you weren't shooting at us all the freaking time."

"I don't think you guys understand what's been done to you," Angel cut in. "Max is a really good leader. What she means is that if you come with us, you can help us stop the people who did this, who experiment on kids. We're going to save the world. Maybe we can work together."

He cackled, and a shiver went down my spine. Why are *evil* kids way creepier than anything else?

"You don't get it, do you? You're forgetting about natural selection," he said. "Trust me—you won't be able to do a thing, when the time comes."

I bristled. "Listen, kid, we can do plenty. If you don't want our help, fine. But don't tell me what I can do." As much as I'd never wanted the whole save-the-world gig, I was irritated that this kid assumed I was totally powerless.

"You're so...Gen 54," he sneered. "You and your bird-kid pals and your doctor pals and the Coalition to Stop the Madness are all trying to save the world." His many little eyes darted back and forth constantly. "But what you don't get is that maybe the world doesn't need to be saved. It can't be."

"I think one person can make a difference," I said. But suddenly I didn't sound so convincing.

"Yeah, and you believe in unicorns and pots of gold at the end of the rainbow," he said. "I'm just telling you how it really is."

"And how do you know 'how it *really* is'?" Dylan asked, stepping closer to me.

"The apocalypse is coming, and no one will be spared," the kid said with scary conviction. "The world will be safe without humans, and every last human will die. And so will you."

I shook with anger and resentment. Everyone — even my mom — had been pushing me to come see these kids, to lead them. Well, clearly, they weren't looking for my help. I was trying to come up with a withering retort when suddenly we heard a series of *pop-pop-pops* and one of them yelled, "*Now!*"

In a flash, the 'noids broke their cord ties, leaped up, and rushed us.

Without hesitation, Dylan, Angel, and I raced to the edge of the roof and threw ourselves off.

29

"I CARE IF you save the world or not, Max," Dylan said softly as we flew back to my mom's house. The tip of his wing brushed mine, and I felt a bolt of electricity.

"Okay, that makes about ten of us," I said, avoiding his eyes. My gaze fell on a little dot moving erratically far below us. An injured animal?

"What's that kid doing down there?" Dylan asked. His exceptional raptor vision was starting to come in pretty handy.

"Looking for the nearest water park?" I said dryly.

"No, I don't think so," Dylan said. He still had a hard time appreciating my sarcasm. I rolled my eyes at Angel. "He's sunburned and staggering. Must be lost."

I glanced around us. The kid was a good five miles

from anything; the chances of his making it to help were pretty slim.

"We should probably just leave him for dead, seeing as how no one actually wants to be saved around here," I grumbled. Okay, it had been a rainy parade back at the Deathwire School for Spider-eyed Kids, and I was feeling bitter. But when I looked up, Dylan grinned at me, and before I knew what was happening, I grinned back.

"Heck, let's go save 'im, whether he wants it or not," Dylan said in his best Scooby-Doo voice, and I laughed. Angel glanced at me, her head cocked.

"What?" I said defensively. "I laugh sometimes."

Long story short, we swooped down on the kid.

Okay, now, if I were staggering and lost in the desert, sunburned and parched and without a hope in the world, and suddenly, three kids with wings fluttered to a graceful landing before me, I'd be pretty sure I was hallucinating or near death or both.

This kid looked up when we landed, blinked, and said, "You again?"

My eyes widened as I plucked recognition from the attic of my brain. "You!" I said.

"You know him?" Dylan asked. "We're in the middle of a desert!"

"I recognize him," I clarified. "We met like forever ago" (six books ago, for those of you in the know) "in the subway tunnels in New York."

"Where's your computer?" I asked. Last time I saw him,

he'd accused us of hacking his precious Mac, which he seemed to consider his only friend on earth.

"I don't need it anymore," the kid said, smiling dreamily.

"Oh yeah?" I said. "Last I knew, you were practically joined at the hip." I mean, not literally, which, sadly, is all too possible in our world. But this was more of a codependent situation.

"I'm free now. The end is near, and soon we'll all be free!" he shouted, raising a fist.

"Again with the world ending," I muttered. The kid had always been a bit off, but it seemed like the heat was really getting to him.

Angel offered him her water bottle, but he shook his head. "Everything's happening, just like my computer predicted." His eyes glazed over. "But I don't need it now. I don't need anything. It's all beautiful, man. Everything will be beautiful once we kill all the humans. You'll see. Can't you feel it?" He looked at me earnestly.

Okay, things were getting more than a little crazy town. "Say what, now?"

"The humans have ruined everything," he said. "But once they're all gone, we can start fresh again. We just need to kill the humans."

"But . . . you're *human!*" said Angel.

His eyes wavered, then focused on her. "Nah, not really."

"Look, you need to get out of the sun, get some fluids into you," I said. "Then you'll quit talking crazy."

"No!" He frowned and shook his head. "You don't understand. You don't want to understand. I have everything I need! I'm being take care of!" He looked off at nothing in the distance. "Everything's being taken care of," he whispered.

"Please, let us help you," I pleaded, taking his arm.

"No!" He pulled away from me and ran off shakily across the hard-packed soil. "I don't need your help! I'm being taken care of!" he shouted over his shoulder.

"Okay, I'm starting to get a complex," I said. "What, I'm not good at saving people anymore?"

The three of us watched the kid stagger away from us. I seriously felt like crying.

"Let's just go home," I said wearily.

30

"AND HOW HAVE you been locating the members of this little ragtag collection of yours?" Maya asked, taking a big swig of Yoo-hoo.

Great. Not only did "Maya" look exactly like Max and have the same husky voice that practically made Fang's knees buckle, but she even talked like Max, all bravado and snark.

"Through my blog," Fang answered. Across the hotel room, the rest of his little ragtag collection actually seemed to be getting along. The new guy, Holden Squibb, had finally arrived, and Kate was explaining to the pale, scrawny kid how she and Star had been kidnapped by two men in lab coats on some school trip. Fang turned back to Maya.

"I started getting letters from kids who were—different. They wanted answers. I want answers too. I thought we could find them together." Maya looked at him when he said "together," and his heart raced. She stepped closer to him, leaning over his shoulder to look at his computer.

"And what've you found?" she said, now inches from his face. Fang kept his eyes locked straight ahead on the screen. He could practically feel the warmth of her skin.

He'd been so stupid. But he'd needed another good fighter on his team and hadn't been sure that the other four would work out. He'd wanted someone…familiar. He'd been a freaking idiot.

Now he didn't know what to do.

"Well, everyone here seems to have been experimented on pretty recently," he said as evenly as he could. "They didn't grow up with it, like we did. They were just regular kids," he said quietly. "And some of them had harsher experiences than others." Fang looked at Holden and frowned. "Anyway, we think it has something to do with these guys." He clicked open a new window, and a banner popped up that read, "Save the Planet. Kill the Humans." Maya gave a low whistle.

"Sweet. These people seem like real winners." Now her lips were close to his ear, and Fang forced himself to breathe normally.

"Yeah, you could say that. They seem to be all for genetically modified kids, though. What they don't get is that not everyone wants to be 'improved.'" He nodded over at

Ratchet, Holden, Kate, and Star. "The gang here joined up because they've got a thing or two to tell the people who did this to them." He squinted at the screen. "If we can just figure out how these Doomsday jerks work..."

"Hmm," said Maya. "Well, I know I can fly, and I know you can fly, but what can they do?" She pointed her bottle at the others. They'd just met, but Ratchet already had Holden in a headlock.

"Ratchet's got, like, insane senses," Fang said, and Ratchet nodded to them from across the room. "Holden can heal really fast, and we think he has the ability to regenerate limbs and stuff."

"Like a starfish," said Maya, nodding. "Cool."

"Yeah," said Fang. "But slightly less cool when you think about how many times they cut him open before the potion actually worked." Fang glanced across the room at Holden's scarred arms and shuddered.

"And the girls, Kate and Star, were injected at the same time, but apparently with different stuff. Seems like the whitecoats screwed with their DNA, just like they did with ours. You wouldn't think it to look at her, but Kate's, like, wicked strong."

He nodded at Star, who was pouring a supersize bag of chips down her throat. "We think Star's part humming-bird or mouse. She can move like lightning, but she burns through about a zillion calories in the process. She must have double the fast-twitch muscle fibers we do since they spliced her genomes."

Maya smiled at him. "I love it when you talk all sciencey."

Fang almost laughed despite himself. He hated talking to people, but maybe with Maya he could just hang. Maybe she could be like Max for him. Like he and Max used to be. Before things got...complicated.

It would be just like before.

31

"MAX! THE MAXALATOR! Maxime! Maxalicious! Maxster!"

Total raced toward me as soon as I landed, wagging his tail. (Oh, just a reminder. Yes, we *are* living in a world where geneticists have messed with dogs too. Total's the first talking dog I've ever met, though—and I hope he's the last.)

"Total! Hi! How was your honeymoon?" I was actually glad to see him. Things had been kind of quiet without him. Relatively.

"I see Mr. Perfect's still hanging around, eh?" he said, drawing together his pointy black Scottie ears. My face flushed as I took a step away from Dylan.

"And Angelkins!" Total licked Angel's face when she

squatted down to pet him, bracing his front paws on her lap.

"Hi, Total," Angel said. "Whoa! Your wings are looking good!"

Total extended his wings proudly, fluttering them a little. "They are, indeed, are they not?" he agreed. "The honeymoon was fantabulous." His eyes got a little misty. "You see before you the happiest of dogs. My Akila and I had a truly magical time. Now she's off visiting her folks, but I missed you, one and all." He looked at me and frowned. "And, of course, I got here just in time to see that everything took a turn for the worse when I left. Everyone looks terrible! I'm gone for a week and—"

"I'm hungry," I said, heading toward the house. "You have any pictures from your honeymoon?"

"I have video!" Total said, happily trotting beside me.

Inside, the flock was a little...different. Besides the limbs in casts and stitched-up wings, everyone had bruises, black eyes, and assorted scrapes, but no one looked at me when I walked in.

"What's going on?" Dylan whispered.

"I was going to ask you the same thing," said Total. "Have they been taking freak pills? Because they're all acting strange."

"Hey, guys," I said, a little too loud. "Everyone okay?"

Nobody moved, not even my mom, who, of all people, I thought I could count on to lead the Max welcoming committee.

"Mom?" I said, walking over to the couch where she was resting. "How's your arm?"

She looked at me, and I felt...empty. I mean, my mom was the person who had taught me that people really can show love through their eyes. Maybe I was imagining things, but she just seemed...different.

"It's okay," she said. "How are you, Max?" She sounded like she didn't care much one way or the other.

"I'm fine," I said. "I'm sorry I stayed out all night. We decided to try to spy on the Gen 77 school, and—"

"Did you find Hans's body?" she said, interrupting me.

"No. We looked, but we ended up finding these spider-eyed 'noid kids, who—"

"That's great, honey. Can you scoot over a bit? I'm trying to watch the news."

Angel, Dylan, and I looked at one another, like *Okayyy,* then we really took in the view:

Nudge, covered in bandages, was lying quietly on the floor by herself, looking miserable.

Gazzy was sitting at a table playing with Ella's old Legos. He was making little people. Not making houses and then exploding them, not blowing things up. Just making little people. Quietly.

Jeb was on crutches, brooding, watching Gazzy from across the room. He looked distraught. Okay, I'll give him a pass since he'd been one breath away from pancaking.

Ella and Iggy were sitting in the kitchen, putting peanut butter and jelly on saltine crackers. Ella was chatting up a storm, and Ig was nodding enthusiastically at her like a bobblehead doll, an idiotic grin on his face. Neither of them even acknowledged my presence.

My heart seized with sudden understanding: the flock was majorly peeved at me for ditching them in the desert.

Dylan sensed that I was on edge and stepped closer to support me. I was freaking out. It would've been so nice just to lean into his warmth...

Instead, I shot him a look that said "I will break your fingers like a nutcracker if you touch me right now" and turned to Angel.

"Ange? Powwow. Stat." I said.

She nodded. I felt a pang of regret when I saw Dylan's hurt face as Angel and I walked out onto the deck, but the flock was my first priority, regardless of those fluttery feelings I kept having that were severely cramping my style.

"Oh, my God," I said as soon as we were outside. "Why didn't you warn me? Is it just me? They're totally giving me the cold shoulder, aren't they? Are they trying to punish me?"

Angel shook her head. "Don't worry, Max. They'll get over it. They're mostly just exhausted and in shock from everything. Something happened between Gazzy and Jeb out there, and I think Gazzy's still reeling, but he's okay."

"But even my mom..."

Angel cocked her head as if she knew something I didn't. "Yeah, something's kind of up with your mom." I tensed, but Angel continued. "I'm way more worried about Ella and Iggy, though."

"Yeah," I huffed. "Could they be any more annoying with all that puppy-eyed sappiness? It's like a barfwich in there."

"No, it's more than that," Angel said. "But I can't quite put my finger on it. It's just—I can always dip into their minds. Not that I do, of course," she added quickly.

"No, of course not," I said.

"They just don't feel like themselves. I mean, they haven't been replaced with clever replicas or bots. It's definitely them. But they're a little—off." She frowned.

"Okay," I said, "Let's find out what the deal is with the Stepford Flock."

32

"MY FRIEND WAS on TV earlier," Ella said, all up in my grill.

She licked peanut butter off her fingers and handed a paper towel to Iggy.

"Oh yeah?" I asked, backing up. "Which friend?"

"Someone from school," she said. "They had this huge rally with all the schools from the district. We talked about the earth and everything that was wrong with it and all the changes that needed to be made," she said, breathless. "You would've loved it, Max. Then we had to stand up and make a pledge if we cared enough about the world to take action, and I stood up, and then they paired us with new friends, and my friend was the best. He told me everything was going to be okay if we just followed his lead, and I believe him, Max. It's going to be beautiful."

"Hey, you know I'm all for fixing the planet," I said. But Ella seemed a little...fanatical all of a sudden.

My mom looked up. "Was that the friend who brought the flyers by?"

"What flyers?" Dylan asked.

"The flyers are an invitation to change," Ella said earnestly.

"Yeah, I can see you've already RSVP'd," I said, eyeing her.

"It's really amazing, Max," said Iggy, waving a couple of bright sheets of colored paper at me. "You have to trust the message and take action. We need to hand these out to everyone we know, so they can join the cause."

I raised an eyebrow. Cynical Iggy wants to "join the cause"? I was officially creeped out.

Angel, Dylan, and I all looked at each other.

"Yeah?" I said, feigning interest. "Let's see 'em."

"Sure," said Robo Iggy.

I unfolded the magenta paper to find pictures of smiling kids and these words:

We know you're special! We know you're one of us. We care about you. Come join us and learn about the message of the One Light.

Brought to you, with love and caring, by the Doomsday Group

" 'Love' and 'caring' and 'Doomsday Group' don't seem to go together," Dylan said, leaning over my shoulder and making the hairs on my neck stand up. "Who's this Doomsday Group, and what are they selling?"

"Basically, they make it sound like a big, ecofriendly glee club," I said. "But it seems a little over the top."

Nudge got up and slunk over, looking absolutely wrecked. "Ella's been ranting about this all afternoon," she whispered. "At first I thought Iggy was just being super-cute and lovey-dovey and humoring her, but since that weirdo came to the door and talked to him, he's started to seem really wonky."

"It's just for kids. This will set us free." Ella's voice, suddenly loud, made me jump. I looked into her glazed eyes, and a shiver ran down my spine. This was...eerily familiar.

"Just for kids?" I asked. She stepped closer to me and so did Iggy. I started to feel a little hemmed in.

"Yeah. 'Cause we're the only ones who can be trusted," Ella said, her eyes sparkling. "The group is meeting at my school tomorrow, and I really want everyone to come. Say you'll come, Max. *Please!*" She was practically shouting at me.

"Yeah, maybe," I said. "It's just that, I mean, it's not the best time for the flock. We're kind of in the middle of something, you know? Hansy's gone, everyone's beat up, and Dylan and I found this hidden school of spider-eyed kids." I couldn't help looking at Dylan and remembering our night spent curled up together on the ledge...

"It's *really* important that you come, Max," Iggy insisted, and now even my name was starting to sound a little creepy. Ella held Iggy's hand and nodded at him encouragingly, then said, "The One Light will set us free."

"And what are you guys going to do with this group?" I asked, feeling like I was talking to Pod People.

Iggy and Ella replied at the exact same time, in the exact same tone of voice. "We're going to save the world," they said, and stepped closer to us.

33

"I THINK I found something," Maya said, looking intently at the computer screen.

The rest of the gang had gone out for lunch, but Fang had wanted to stay behind to research the Doomsday Group and update his blog. More news stories on the group had been popping up by the hour, and the Internet was exploding with posts about this hip new "earth cleanse."

To his surprise, Maya had volunteered to stay with him.

"Check it out. These aren't whitecoats, Fang. They're kids. All of them."

"No way." Fang leaned over her shoulder, reminding himself to keep it light. They were just doing research. He didn't have to think about her sweet smile or the sound of her voice.

"Seriously," she scrolled down. "I'm getting hits for 'Doomsday Group' literally all over the globe. It's gone viral on the Net just since yesterday." She opened a new window. "And check this out. All these kids are posting about the enhanced generation. They're babbling about a future world of clones," she whispered. "It's so messed up."

Fang nodded, raising his wings a little. "I get it. Believe me."

"You actually don't get it," Maya said, turning away from him. "You think we're alike because we've both been genetically engineered, because we both have wings." She got up and began pacing. "But I'm a clone. Can you even fathom what that's like? To be made from someone else? Someone who still exists?"

Fang's throat felt dry. What was he supposed to say?

"You *are* different, Maya. You can still be you," he said lamely. She laughed bitterly — clearly, that hadn't been the right thing to say.

"You mean I can be *her*," she said. He started to protest, but she shook her head. "I've seen those brooding looks. And you know...you're great." Fang felt a pang. "But do you think I don't know why you look at me that way? I know you want me to be her. Everyone has always wanted me to be her. But I can't. I'm just...me."

She looked up at him seeming totally vulnerable despite

how amazingly powerful she was. But she was right. She'd always be a bit like Max to him. And Fang, despite his wrecked heart, almost couldn't keep himself from kissing her. Thankfully, before he could screw up in such a royal way, the gang burst through the door, howling and armed with...

Cheez Whiz.

34

I TOOK A big step back and found myself against a wall. "Whoa!" I said, holding up my hand like a traffic cop. Pod-Ig and Pod-El stopped. I smiled. "Give me a little space here. Please. I need room to read this stuff." I turned the flyer over, and they edged away.

"We're going outside again for a sec. Maybe you guys should go tell Gazzy about saving the world," I suggested. "He didn't look totally convinced." Ella nodded eagerly. I felt kinda bad for sicking her on the Gasman, but if he'd been immune to her brainwashing up till now, I figured he was safe.

I watched through the window as they drifted toward the kitchen. My knees were shaking, and I could feel my heart racing.

"So, we're all agreed that the lovebirds are totally, like, programmed, right?" I huffed.

"Affirmative," Total said, nodding.

I sighed, annoyed. "So basically, in the middle of all this other crap, we've gotta go take out Ella's flyer-wielding 'friend.' I have a can of whoop-butt at the ready for the cool kid who sucked out my family's brains," I said.

"Agreed," said Dylan.

"So, we should go to the school tomorrow, right?" asked Angel. "Ella said everyone was going to meet these guys."

"Yep," I said glumly. I mean, I don't go to school voluntarily as it is. So to go so I could track down the people who had sucked out my family's brains made school even less appealing, if that's possible.

"And Max," said Angel, ever the bearer of bad news. "There's something else."

"Something else besides this?" I didn't know how much more I could take.

"Are you talking about that video?" Total asked. Angel whirled around and glared at him.

"What video?" I asked.

"Fang's . . . blog," Total whispered, licking a paw casually, the way he did when he was embarrassed.

My jaw dropped. "Someone had better start talking!"

35

"WHAT VIDEO?" I asked again, my eyes like daggers.

Total flopped down on his belly and rested his head on his paws.

"Angel?" I pressed.

"I may have seen something on Fang's blog," she admitted reluctantly.

"And you didn't tell me?!"

"You made us promise never to mention his name!" she said. I hate it when they throw unhelpful details in my face.

Dylan stepped away looking a little wounded, and I actually had to keep myself from pulling him back toward me. As if I didn't have enough to deal with—now my heart felt like it had been run through a meat grinder.

I gritted my teeth. "Show me."

Angel went in the house to get our laptop, then brought it outside. I watched over her shoulder as she called up Fang's blog and clicked on a video link. I held my breath while it played. It was grainy, poor quality, like it had been shot on someone's cell phone. It showed a hotel room and several older kids sitting around, some watching the news on TV in the background. I stared at their faces but hadn't seen one of them before.

Then Fang and someone else came into the picture. The camera panned up to reveal her face, and I gasped. There I was, in a strange hotel room! Fang was grinning in that slightly crooked way that made my heart beat faster, and I grinned back and aimed a can of Cheez Whiz at him. He playfully opened his mouth, and the other kids laughed. Then the on-screen me actually shot Cheez Whiz into his mouth. We laughed some more, then I shot Cheez Whiz into my own mouth.

Except that it had never happened. I had no memory of that day. Weirdly, on the TV they were watching, the date that had flashed in front of the news was…today. Just a few hours ago.

I stared at Angel. "And I don't remember this cute little scene because…?" Then it hit me, before she even answered. And my stomach dropped down somewhere around my knees.

"Max II."

Angel nodded and paused the video.

I stared at the computer screen, my face frozen, laughing into Fang's face. He was looking at her exactly the way he used to look at me. I hadn't thought I could possibly feel worse about the whole Fang fiasco, but I'd been wrong.

Not only had he left, but he'd replaced me. Like, immediately. Replaced me with an exact copy of me. How unfair was that? I mean, even if I could replace Fang with an identical but more reasonable copy of Fang, I wou—

"What's that?" Dylan pointed at the computer.

I blinked, feeling like I'd been dipped into a fresh vat of pain. My gaze numbly followed his finger, then I saw the small TV screen in the background.

"What?" I could barely get the word out. I just wanted to go stand in a hot shower and not think.

"Look," said Dylan.

"Oh, my gosh," said Angel. She let the video resume.

I swallowed and tried to focus. Then I saw it: on the TV in Fang's hotel room was a breaking news report. The headline was "The Doomsday Group: The Earth or Us?"

Fang pointed at the TV and said something I couldn't make out. The other kids nodded.

Dylan, Angel, and I looked at one another. I felt like we were the only sane people left in a crazy, unpredictable world. Which means you should be afraid. Very, very afraid.

"What's going on?" I wondered aloud, frustrated.

"Whatever it is, it looks like Fang wants to find out too," said Angel.

I clenched my jaw. "Okay. Tomorrow. School."

36

"BUT WHY ARE you going if we can't go?" Nudge asked for the third time.

I covered my eyes with my hands, trying to relieve my throbbing headache. I had gotten practically no sleep last night, what with everybody acting like Pod People and then seeing Fang and his Max replacement living it up online. Plus, Total had insisted on staying at the foot of my bed, and he talked in his sleep—about his honeymoon. Frankly, TMI.

"You know why, Nudge," I said under my breath. "I need to see what's making the kids all Looney Tunes, get to the root of this Boom Boom Cult." I saw Ella eyeing me from across the room. "I'm really interested in learning about their cause," I said loudly, trying to sound sincere, which, let's face it, is a stretch for me.

"Angel and Dylan are going," Nudge pointed out.

"Angel can read minds," I said under my breath again. "Might be useful for getting in. And I . . . need Dylan there. For support." He gave me one of his dazzling smiles from across the room. I wolfed down a banana, ignoring the critical look on Nudge's face.

"Nudge can come!" zombie Ella piped up. "Everyone can come. The Doomsday Group will set us free."

"Yeah, yeah. Everything's going to be beautiful. We get it. They're not coming." I turned to Nudge, lowering my voice. "Look, they got to Ella and Iggy. They could get to you too. It's too risky if we all go."

"But you already left us once," Nudge whined. "Gazzy's staring into space, all traumatized from almost letting Jeb die, and I don't want to stay here alone. *Please.* I need you, Max."

She sure knew how to rip my heart out and stomp all over it.

"I'm really sorry, kiddo," I said, my voice softening. "I know you guys have had a rough couple of days. But you won't be alone. My mom's here. Jeb's here. Gazzy's here."

"I'm here. What, don't I count?" Total said, sulking.

"See, you've got Total too. We'll be back soon," I told Nudge. "Let's jet, kids."

Ella attended a local public school. The campus consisted of a bunch of one-story buildings painted white that were clustered around a big courtyard, with footpaths leading from one building to the next. As schools go, it wasn't awful. I didn't know what I expected to find, San Quentin? Considering our history with schools, that wasn't much of a stretch for me.

For a few moments we stood in front of the school, mapping the layout in our minds. Ella and Iggy were holding hands, which would have been kind of adorable if they weren't all dead-eyed and brainsucked. Then the front door of one of the buildings opened, and we braced ourselves.

I looked at Dylan. "I've got your back," we both said together. He laughed, and I rolled my eyes. Partly at him and partly at myself for feeling all fluttery again.

Students and the occasional teacher began to stream out through the door, moving quietly into the courtyard. Every one of them was smiling and content-looking, if not grinning like a hyena. These were mainly teenagers, people. It was gross.

"Okay," I whispered to Dylan and Angel. "Let's spread out. Keep your wits about you, and avoid becoming zombified or whatever. Let's do this."

The kids gathered in groups or in pairs. I heard a lot of talk about caring for the planet and saving the world, but, come on, there had to be more to it than that.

"Hello," one girl said to me brightly, grabbing both of my hands. These people did not grasp the concept of personal space.

"Hello," I said, mimicking her cheery tone, which, I bet you've already guessed, was not superconvincing.

"I'm so glad you came to orientation!" She beamed at me.

"Uh, yeah," I said. "No prob. Doomsday's been my specialty for, like, ever."

She cocked her head, her eyes boring into mine. "Do you want to be my friend? I want to be your friend. We need you to follow the One Light. With an earth cleanse, we'll all be free. We need you to accept the message and join us. Do you accept it?"

She blinked like a possessed doll, and I looked around. Where was Angel? And Dylan? "Let's back up a smidge. Remind me what the message is."

"The message is —"

"Max!" Dylan called me over.

"Hold that thought," I wriggled out of the girl's grasp and found Dylan talking to a tall boy with a Zac Efron smile.

"Josh, this is Max. Max, Josh is going to get us more flyers to hand out." Dylan had the glass-eyed, cocked-head look down perfectly. With his movie-star looks, pearly white smile, and smooth face, it was seriously creepy. It almost seemed like...

I raised an eyebrow at him, and he stuck out his tongue and crossed his eyes when Josh turned away from us to grab the flyers. It was such a dorky move that I should have felt sorry for him, but it was genuinely...cute. *Focus, Max!* I mentally kicked myself. This was not exactly the time to get mushy.

"Here you guys go." Josh loaded our arms with the colorful stacks of paper. "Remember, we need to make sure everyone joins," he looked at us earnestly. "We have to save the planet."

The gathering was starting to pulse and get louder, kids shouting stuff about beauty and freedom. All eeriness aside, what they were saying didn't actually sound that bad. Wasn't this what my own mission had been for years and years?

"Tell me, Josh, do you know who the flyers came from in the first place? Who's in charge around here?" I asked.

"They came from the One Light," he said. "You know that."

"Oh, yeah," I mumbled. We had to figure out this whole One Light business, ASAP.

Everyone is affected, Angel broke into my thoughts from across the square. *I'm getting bombarded with thoughts, and they're all jumbled, chaotic, violent.* She looked over at me, panic in her eyes. *But Max, this is big. Worse than genocide. We're talking humanicide. Total extermination!*

I looked around for my own zombies. Ella was chanting, then she pumped a fist in the air, which a bunch of kids instantly copied. I tried to get to her, but Botboy Josh grabbed my arm, hard, and stepped closer to me, flashing those crazy eyes.

"I don't think you want to do that, Hoss," Dylan growled, sounding like he might go grizzly on the kid. Josh's smile never faltered, but he let go of me, and I spun around toward the mob, trying to see where Ella had gone. I was taller than many of these kids, but when I got up on tiptoe and peered around, I still couldn't see my sister's dark head anywhere. She'd been swallowed up.

I spotted Iggy just a few yards away, though, so I nodded at Dylan, and we made our way toward him.

"The Doomsday Group is the hope of tomorrow," someone said, and there were shouts of agreement. Another kid said, "Save the planet!" Then somebody added, "Kill the humans."

Something in my brain finally clicked, and then it seemed so freaking obvious. The 'noids back at the school. The delirious kid in the desert. "The Earth or Us." And now these kids. Desert Boy was right: the end was near.

"Kill the humans," Iggy shrieked, unfolding his giant wings.

"Oh, Ig," I whispered. "No."

37

"WE NEED TO get out of here, now," Dylan said under his breath.

But the cult was already swarming around Iggy.

"He's the new generation," I heard someone say. "He's the future." It was like they wanted him to be their leader.

"Iggy! Iggy!" kids were chanting, closing in on us. They were touching his face, stroking his wings. "He's the future."

Some girls sobbed as if he were Robert Pattinson or something. "I want to be you," they said, weeping, their painted-on smiles making the whole scene even weirder. "Can you sign my flyer?"

"I'll take out my eyes," one psycho volunteered happily. "I want to be blind like Iggy."

"This is bad," Angel said next to me. "Max, this is really, *really* bad." I gave her a look that said, "Like, *you think?!*"

Normally, I follow the "no birdkid or flock relative left behind" rule. For all I knew, Ella was about to gouge out her eyes too. But I was being swept up in a crowd of insane, horrifying zombies, all chanting about saving the planet and murdering about seven billion people to do it.

So I made a fast, horrible decision.

"On the count of three, we grab Iggy and blow this popsicle stand," I yelled. "One, two, three!"

Dylan, Angel, and I broke away from the group and pounded across the school parking lot until we had room to jump in the air to get aloft. This, obviously, prompted a new round of murmurs about us being the future, which we'd heard before, but it felt a bit less...flattering than it usually did.

Dylan and I swooped over Iggy, grabbed him under the arms, and lifted him up, just like the flying monkeys did to Dorothy in Oz.

"Let me go," Iggy said. "I am the future!" He squirmed a bit and kicked his legs. I held on tighter. He's tall but superskinny, so we could carry him without too much trouble.

I sighed. "Right now, Ig, the Magic 8 Ball of your future says 'Signs point to nutso.'"

Angel scanned the ground below. "I don't see Ella anywhere!"

"I can't believe we just...left her there," Dylan said. I

shot him a look. I was the flock leader. I knew I'd made the right call in the moment, and I didn't need anyone's approval. But it still stung not to have him on my side.

"Maybe, just maybe, we can convince Mom and Jeb to come back and get Ella," I said. "First, though, let's get Iggy away from that creepy crowd!"

"They weren't creepy," Iggy said, trying to flail. "They want to build a new society, a better society, after the world ends. And all we have to do is kill all the humans." He smiled up at us.

"Okay," I said. "I'm picking up on a couple of problem phrases. Like, 'after the world ends' and the 'kill all the humans' part."

"There's no problem," Iggy said.

"We have to deprogram him!" Angel yelled frantically.

Iggy blinked and, with his face still blank and happy, babbled about killing everyone. I couldn't even see my Iggy anymore. It was terrifying.

We'll save you, Ig. If you're in there, we'll save you.

38

IGGY HUNG LIMPLY between Dylan and me, like he'd forgotten he could fly too. At last, my mom's house came into view, and we began our descent. When I saw Total out front waiting for us, my stomach knotted up.

"Where's Ella?" he asked right away.

"We lost her in the mob of zombies at the school," I reported. "My mom and Jeb need to go back and get her while we deprogram Iggy."

Total shook his shaggy black head. "Not long after you left, your mom and Jeb disappeared. Nudge and Gazzy didn't even seem to notice they left — both of them are still here."

"They left? Where did they go?" I asked. "Did they take the car?"

"That's the weird thing," said Total. "They walked out.

After a couple minutes, I thought, 'Hey, maybe I should check on 'em,' you know? So I went out. The car's still here, but I couldn't find them anywhere. I even flew around and searched the whole area. It's like a spaceship picked them up or something."

I looked into his bright black eyes and saw worry there.

"Crap," I said and went inside. In the living room, Nudge and Gazzy were sitting on the couch watching news stories that featured—you guessed it—the Dooms-day Group. After one brief mention yesterday, the Doomsday Group now dominated the coverage on every news channel.

"One Light," Iggy said serenely, reaching toward the TV.

"Okay, we've got to get him back from never-never land," I said. "Angel, can you get in his head, sort of do a reset?"

Angel sighed. "I told you. I've been in his head. It's jumbled up, just like the minds of the rest of those kids at the rally. Everything's a mishmash. I don't even know how to untangle all the weird thoughts."

"What kind of weird thoughts?" Dylan asked.

"It's more like pictures, like dreams, sort of," Angel tried to explain. "But as soon as I try to follow one thing, it slips away."

"Kill the humans!" Iggy yelled.

"Those kind of weird thoughts, apparently," I said. "He's just too way out right now. In the movies, they always throw people in cold showers to make them calm down. Think that'd work?"

Angel gave me a look. "Max, when has Iggy ever been docile about taking a shower?" She had a point, but it was worth a shot anyway. We didn't exactly have a backup plan.

It wasn't pretty. It took all three of us to get Iggy into the tub and turn on the cold water. Then Iggy went haywire. He bolted like a wild horse and tried to leap out. Dylan and I grabbed him, using all our strength to wrestle him back under the shower.

"What are you doing?" Iggy wailed in a voice I'd never heard before, as if the water were acid. "What are you doing?"

He seemed terrified, but the three of us fought to hold him under the shower while he thrashed around.

"Stop! Stop!" Iggy yelled, tears running down his cheeks. He was drenched, like the rest of us, his reddish-blond hair flopping to one side. Tiny water droplets clung to his eyelashes, and his cheeks were flushed. "What's happening?!"

"I don't know!" I shouted.

"You're killing me!" Iggy shrieked, hardly sounding human. He writhed and moaned, wrenching his body back and forth.

"I'm dying!" Iggy wailed, his hands clawing at the side of the tub. "I'm dying!!"

I was seriously freaked. I mean, all the kids hated taking showers, but I'd never seen anything like this.

Then Iggy suddenly slumped down in the tub, his eyes closed.

"Oh, my God!" I panicked. "Turn it to warm water, Dylan—now!"

"I'm getting in," Angel whispered as the water temperature rose. "Lines of communication are opening up, and if I work at these crazy knots of death thoughts, I can break through to him. He's still freaking out, but there doesn't seem to be the same level of resistance."

Then he twitched.

"Iggy…" I held my breath.

He blinked slowly and shook the water out of his eyes.

"What…what are you doing?" he asked, sounding kind of groggy. Groggy…a lot like the old Iggy.

My eyes brightened, and Dylan and Angel and I all exchanged hopeful glances.

"Iggy?" I asked again.

"Yeah?" He blinked, wiping his face with one hand. "What are you guys doing? If you wanted me to take a shower, all you had to do was pay me ten bucks, like you usually do." He ran one hand through his hair, making it stand up in wet peaks.

I let out a deep breath and looked at Angel: her face was beaming. She looked at me and nodded—his thoughts were back to normal.

"So what's going on?" he demanded, sitting up a bit.

"How do you feel?" I asked.

"Like a wet dog," he answered irritably. "What's wrong with you guys?"

39

"I WON'T DO IT," Star said.

"Then I guess this whole trust exercise has failed," Fang said mildly. The gang had fun together earlier—he'd forgotten how simultaneously repulsive and delicious Cheez Whiz could be—but within minutes they were all at each other's throats again.

Max used to threaten and bully people into working together. But that approach quit having the desired effect long before Fang had left. He needed to do something different, something better.

So, he Googled "team building." Which, he discovered, really meant a rousing little game of Never Have I Ever.

"I don't even know how to play," Holden Squibb complained.

Ratchet cackled. "That's 'cause you're a baby, Starfish, even if you can regenerate limbs and stuff. What are you, like, twelve?" Holden glared at Ratchet.

"Cut it out, guys," Fang said. "Look, we're six really different people. But we need to work together as a team, or we'll all end up dead." The surprise on their faces made Fang think that maybe the word *dead* was a bit too strong. But he knew what he had said could possibly be true.

"All you have to do is say 'Never have I ever…' and fill in the blank. Then anyone in the group who's done it has to raise their hand, including you, if you've actually done it. If you want to reveal something about yourself, say something you've done. If you don't want to reveal anything personal, say something that you think someone else in the group might've done. Cool?" Fang sighed. He felt like a camp counselor or something. It was exhausting.

But to his surprise, everyone formed a circle, even if they did roll their eyes.

"Great. I'll start," Fang said. He sure hated being the leader all the time. *Why did Angel always want this job so much?* he wondered. "Never have I ever…played a team-building game as stupid as this before." Maya smiled, but everyone else's eyes shot daggers at him as he raised his hand.

"Never have I ever…gotten mistaken for a ten-year-old when I was almost fifteen," Ratchet said, and no one budged.

Star shoved Holden into the center of the circle. "I think that's you, squirt."

"Never have I ever...owned a designer bag," Holden quipped in response, and Star glared, raising her hand.

Fang made himself count backward from twenty by threes.

"Never have I ever...had Cheez Whiz up my nose, in my hair, and between my toes at the same time," Maya said. Everyone laughed, and they all shot up their hands.

"Never have I ever...played down my strength so no one would look at me funny," Kate said, holding up her hand.

"Never have I ever...been seriously hungry all day every day because I can't get enough calories to sustain energy," Star said, raising her hand along with Fang and Maya.

"Never have I ever...accidentally chopped off my finger and watched it grow back," Holden said, and mimed hacking his finger off, resulting in a few chuckles and a cry of "Yeah, Starfish!" from Ratchet.

Maya spoke up, her eyes shining at Fang from across the circle. "Never have I ever...felt the wind whip through my hair as I soared twenty thousand feet up with only my wings to carry me." They both raised their hands.

"Never have I ever...been thrown out of my house for being a freak," Ratchet said quietly and raised his hand. Across the room, Star raised her hand too, and they stood like that for a few seconds, just looking at each other.

"Never have I ever...been injected with hypodermic needles and locked in a cage," Fang said. Every single hand went up, and as they looked around the room, everyone seemed to really get each other for the first time. They had all been abused, and they all needed the same help.

"Never have I ever...received a message telling me that I had to help save the world," Maya said, staring deeply into Fang's eyes. He looked back at her, and she nodded almost imperceptibly. His hand slowly went up.

No one, not even Max, knows about that.... He felt a faint shiver run down his spine.

"So...you want to do something about the Doomsday Group, or what?" Holden asked.

Fang nodded. "I read that they're holding a big rally in San Diego, starting tomorrow," Fang said. "It'll be at Comic-Con, that huge convention. I don't know how the DG will fit in with that, but I think it's the first thing we should check out."

"If it means we can get to the butchers who experimented on us, who cut us up, I'm all for it," Kate said.

Holden nodded, rubbing the scars on his arms.

"Let's take 'em down," Ratchet said, and Star actually smiled.

"So...San Diego?" Fang asked.

"San Diego!" the gang agreed.

40

AFTER A DAY of zombified culties shrieking about wiping out the human race and an hour of hysterical panic holding Iggy down while fighting for his mind as he writhed in the bathtub, I'd aged about five years, and I swear I got my first gray hair from that ordeal.

However, we were now back on track. We were six normalish birdkids, one of whom had recently endured a freezing cold deprogramming experience, and a small black dog thrilled that he'd escaped a bath. Together we sat, a little freaked out, around the table, trying to plan our next course of action.

"Dr. Martinez, Jeb, and Ella are still gone," Dylan said, and Gazzy countered with, "Well, *duh*." I was glad to hear the Gasman sounding almost back to normal after the whole not-talking-for-two-days thing, which I hadn't really had time to deal with.

"Do you want to saddle up, go back, and get Ella?" Dylan asked me, ignoring Gazzy.

"That's my first instinct," I said slowly, thinking. "But I'm really worried about what this Doomsday Group is up to. If it's something serious, we might have to try to stop it. Fast. This thing is spreading like the plague."

"It's just so weird that—" Nudge began, then stopped after a harsh look from Angel.

"What?" I said.

Nudge pressed her lips together and looked away. Total coughed meaningfully.

I sighed and rubbed my temples. "Just tell me. Obviously, it's about Fang." I was amazed I could even say his name without having to curl up into a little ball afterward.

"Well, it's just so weird that we're dealing with the Doomsday Group here, and Fang is going to California to do the same thing," Nudge said quickly.

I'd seen mention of the Doomsday Group on the TV in the little stomach-turning video I'd seen of Fang and his Max stand-in but didn't know it was more than that.

"Fang mentioned them in his blog?" I demanded.

"Yeah," Nudge admitted.

I sat down at the laptop and called up Fang's blog myself, for the first time since he'd left. It was painful, just seeing the words he'd written. I was aware of Dylan, who'd gone across the room and was sitting moodily on the sofa, flicking through TV channels.

" 'So, Comic-Con!' " I read, as Total stretched up to my lap. " 'I've always wanted to go! Looks like I'll get my chance—the Doomsday Group is holding a huge rally there. Why, I don't know, but the Fang gang is on its way. Feel free to drop by! I'll be the one with real—not strap-on—wings.' "

I looked up. "No one was going to tell me about this because…"

Nudge looked uncomfortable. "You made us all promise never to mention his name," she whispered, and I winced as that sentence came back to bite me in the butt again. "Plus, you were busy dealing with Iggy who was, you know, brainsucked," she said.

I sat back. "So the DG is going to have a big rally at Comic-Con."

"We are so there!" Total said. "I'm definitely getting Tricia Helfer's autograph!"

We all turned to look at him. "What?" he said. "She's hot. For a human."

"If the DG is having a huge rally, we should go," Dylan agreed, which was big of him, especially since he knew Fang would be there too.

Inside, my heart raced at the thought of possibly seeing Fang again. Did he know how much he was hurting me by advertising the new Fang gang? Was he really that cruel, to post videos of himself with his Max stand-in? Was he deliberately trying to hurt me?

That didn't sound like Fang. But I didn't know what to think.

"But what about Ella and my mom and Jeb?" I asked.

"I've been thinking about that," said Gazzy. The serious tone of his voice made me look at him sharply.

"What's up, Gaz?" Nudge asked.

"Well, before the crash, when I was trying to hold Jeb and then he let go?" Gazzy's face showed how painful the memory was. "Right as I knew I couldn't hold him much longer, he yelled one last thing, the last thing he wanted me to know before he died."

As much as I usually hated Jeb, I couldn't help admitting that I really did want to know what his almost-last words were. "And that was...?"

"He said, 'The human race will have to die to save the planet. Just like I have to die to save you.'" Gazzy looked up, his blue eyes troubled. "I think maybe Jeb is in on it. Your mom too."

41

"WHA-HUH?" I SAID, already bristling. My mom? In on a heinous conspiracy?

"I know, I know," Gazzy said quickly. "You know how great I think Dr. M is. I don't want her to be in on this."

"Jeb, okay," I said, my temper flaring. "He's a lying, two-faced weasel. But my mom's good. She's always been good to us, and now you're just selling her out?"

"But...your mom *trusts* Jeb," said Gazzy. "Even after you thought he had betrayed you and us and cut off all ties with him, your mom stayed in touch with him."

That had really ticked me off, but I figured she'd had her reasons. Like maybe she thought weasels were really cute. Or could be trained to do circus tricks.

"Something else," Dylan said, sounding reluctant. "Dr. Martinez is incredible. She's helped us all and even welcomed me into her home. But she also let Jeb bring Dr. Hans here without warning anyone, even after what you told her about him. Even after he almost killed Fang. She let him come here. Didn't that bother you at all?"

I spun around to look at him. "Oh, now everyone wants to jump on the traitor train to jerkville. You've been here for what? Two seconds?! This is *my mom* we're talking about!"

He put a hand on my shoulder, and I stiffened. I opened my mouth to continue defending my mom, who is, as I've pointed out, the only mom I'm ever likely to have. But despite my little outburst, a tiny seed of doubt had taken root in me. Dylan's instincts were usually pretty spot-on. And he always had my back, except for the whole leaving-Ella-behind-in-a-sea-of-cult-freaks thing.

I looked up and expected to find hurt or anger on his face, but he just looked sorry. And like he really cared about me. And then that rarest of rare things happened: I felt bad.

Then I looked at the concerned faces of my flock. So many times in the past, I'd ignored what they'd said and charged ahead, my mind made up about how it was going to be. But they weren't saying this stuff just to mess with me or to make me feel bad. I shut my mouth abruptly and sat down.

"Wasn't it your mom who convinced us all to go see the Gen 77 kids that morning?" Angel asked gently. "You didn't want to go, and we were all on your side. But your mom said she'd like to go, and that's why all of us got in Jeb's plane. Which is why we almost died."

I felt like I'd been punched in the stomach really hard. Everything in me wanted to tell them they were wrong, they were crazy. But the truth was that, as much as I loved my mom, and as much as I trusted her, I'd still known her for just a few years, and she was a grown-up. We didn't have such a great track record with adults in general or with scientists in particular. Even though it really, really hurt, I trusted the flock with my heart, with my gut.

I had to think this one through and not go charging off.

Maybe I really am getting older and perhaps a tiny bit wiser.

"But my mom and Jeb got on the plane too," I pointed out half heartedly.

Dylan said, "Maybe they figured that with all of us there, you and me and the rest of the flock, there was no way we'd let them die. If the accident was planned, and Hans somehow escaped out the front of the plane before it hit the ground, maybe they knew that we would come through for them somehow."

I tried taking some slow, deep breaths. I didn't, couldn't, believe that my mom would really put us on a plane she thought would crash. But they were right—something was sketchy. My stomach was in knots. My chest hurt.

"Maybe Jeb kidnapped my mom?" I suggested hopefully.

"She does love you, Max," Angel said, crossing over to me. "She absolutely does. I can feel it. But everyone involved with the Doomsday Group seems to put the situation above the people, you know? Like, the end of the world is bigger than who loves who or who wants to be with whomever. Maybe she—maybe they're all still convinced that they're acting for the greater good."

"Argh," I said, covering my eyes with my hands, the blank faces of the Doomsday zombies flashing before me. "There's nothing more dangerous than someone trying to act for the greater good." I took a deep breath and exhaled slowly. I looked at the floor, at my feet, anywhere but at the caring faces of my flock. I wanted to crawl into a little hole and not have to deal with any of this.

Then, with my next breath, I got angry again. This was my fault. This was what I got for trusting people, for letting them in. My mom was my weak spot, and I had been stupid! Naive! What had I been thinking?

I stood up, my face determined. "Maybe you guys are right. I hope we're all wrong. But until we know that, until I can really believe that, we need to close ranks right now, to protect ourselves."

"What do you mean, Max?" Nudge asked.

"I mean we should make a pact, today. A pact that from now on, no matter what, we will never again trust a grown-up."

Nudge's eyes got big, and even Dylan looked surprised.

I held out my fist. One by one, they each made fists and stacked them on top of mine. Then Total pushed a paw up under my hand. I tapped Iggy's hand twice, he tapped Gazzy's, and so on, until we had all agreed. And that was that.

This had been quite the year for heartbreak and disillusionment.

42

"OKAY, NO GROWN-UPS," Gazzy said. "What now?"

"Ella," I said. "She's not a grown-up. If she's in on every-thing, we need to pump her for information. If she's inno-cent, we need to save her."

"Of course she's innocent!" Iggy said, and I remem-bered how he'd been cuddling up to her like a puppy dog these last couple weeks. I looked at him apologetically.

"Yeah but, I mean, just in case," I said, looking around, "we should ransack the place for clues. Spread out!"

We all scattered as if pawing through someone else's stuff was the most fun we'd had in weeks. But an hour later, we gathered in the kitchen, still no closer to an answer.

"I found this, though," Gazzy said excitedly, holding up

a small green box. "Gas-X! Like, 'X' for explosion! This is great! I'm thinking I rig this with a detonator, and—"

"Did you find that in the medicine cabinet?" Dylan asked.

"Yeah."

"It's for upset stomachs," Dylan said, trying to hide a smile. He pointed to the words on the box. "It's to reduce gas in your digestive system, not to create more gas to make explosions."

Gazzy's face fell as Iggy said, "Really? Gazzy, take it! Take the whole box!"

"I second that emotion!" said Total.

"Okay," I said sharply. "Moving on. Did anyone else find anything?"

Iggy looked sheepish. "I found this," he said, holding up a cell phone. "It's Ella's. I felt bad going through her stuff, but if it'll help us find her..."

It took Nudge about a minute and a half to hack into the phone and bypass the security codes.

"She's slipping," Gazzy said, checking his watch.

"Am not!" Nudge said crossly. "It's overlaid with extra protection. It's weird. But I think I'm in. Hang on." She got a small cord and connected the phone to our laptop.

"Okay, now we'll all be able to see everything in the phone," she said, pointing to the computer screen.

A bunch of patchwork gibberish shot across the monitor, and I was reminded of that computer guy, the one we'd just seen in the desert. His computer had done stuff like this when we'd first met him in the subway tunnels.

"Slow it down," I said, as Nudge's fingers flew across the keyboard.

The images suddenly halted, and Nudge started scrolling through them.

"Well, look at that," said Dylan.

We saw photographs of the Gen 77 facility Dylan and I had gone to the day before. There were floor plans, all labeled, and photos of the interior and exterior of the building.

"What?" said Iggy. "What is it?"

"That weird facility Max and I checked out," Dylan said, pointing. "And there are those spider-eyed kids."

We also saw a couple of pictures of what looked like a cafeteria. I suppose even Gen 77 kids had to eat. I followed Dylan's finger to the images of our pals, the many-eyed fighters.

There were also text messages about meetings and a ton of background banners repeating the phrases "The Earth or Us" and "Kill the Humans." There was even a motivational video of some chick with a hypnotic voice and really beautiful eyes.

"Let's see what other pearls of propaganda the cult sent to Ella," I said.

Nudge expertly turned the innards of Ella's phone inside out, which revealed a bunch of scientific gibberish about unraveling DNA strands and inserting alternate DNA and RNA into the them. It sounded eerily familiar. Like we-were-injected-with-bird-DNA-and-raised-in-cages familiar. Angel raised an eyebrow at me, reading my thoughts, and I remembered her panicked message at Ella's school about humanicide.

I sat back and let out a long breath. "Well, I guess we've got a date with doom," I said melodramatically.

"What do you mean?" Dylan asked.

"Looks like Ella's definitely at the facility. If she's all cute and cuddly with the Doomsday Group, we have to go save her, even if she tries to eat our brains," I said. "We leave in five minutes."

43

"WHOA! WHAT'S DOWN there?" Dylan pointed to a small flame on the ground, about a mile away. The six of us, plus Total, had set off from my mom's house and headed southeast when it was already getting dark, and now we were about five or six miles from the Gen 77 facility.

I peered closer, then remembered Dylan's vision was way better than mine. "You're asking *me?*" I said.

"Looks like a campfire." He squinted. "Bunch of people sitting around it."

"My guess is a hellions' hootenanny," I said, and Dylan chuckled. "A what?"

He shook his head. Even in the dark, I could sense his rather, um, *adorable* smirk. "Let's check it out," he said, and we started down, the others following.

Anyone looking up and paying attention would have seen us, seven dark silhouettes against the moon. But these people weren't paying attention to us. They were gathered around their campfire, singing songs and roasting marshmallows. We circled silently overhead, descending lower and lower, and I think we all spotted her at almost the same time.

"Ella!" Total shouted but shut up pretty quick when I elbowed him in his furry ribs. The culties seemed too lobotomized to notice.

My half sister was sitting there, holding a skewered marshmallow over the fire, singing along with the others. I didn't recognize the song. They'd put new words to something traditional, and it took several minutes for me to make out the refrain:

"We'll all go out together when we go
Yes, we'll all go out together when we go
Oh, how the world will die
In great fire from the sky
Yes, we'll all go out together when we go."

"Call me old-fashioned," Total huffed, "but I'll take 'She'll Be Coming Round the Mountain' over that anytime."

"Yeah," said Nudge. "I mean, grim much?"

We climbed about a thousand feet so we could talk normally. "Ig, have I told you lately how happy I am to have you back from loony land?" I said. He smiled, but it was clear he was really shaken up about Ella. "Okay, flock. Suggestions?"

"A raid!" Gazzy said. "A blitz! I'll make a diversion, a little ways away, you guys swoop down, grab her—"

"They're pretty far away from the facility, but we don't want to do anything that might show up on surveillance," I interrupted him.

"Basic hand-to-hand combat?" Dylan suggested.

"That would work, but then we'd have a bunch of beaten-up kids with stories to tell," I pointed out.

"I have an idea," said Iggy.

44

AND SO IT WAS that the Great White Spirit descended from the heavens and appeared to the lost pilgrims in the desert.

Iggy floated gently down through the smoke. With the firelight shining on him and smoke plumes wreathing around his head and wings, he did sort of look like a scruffy angel. You know, if God had a sense of humor about it.

Now, Iggy is nearly six feet tall and superskinny. He has really pale skin, reddish-blond hair, and practically colorless blue eyes (when he takes off his shades). Basically, he looks kind of freaky even without the fourteen-foot wings. So to see him coming down from the sky, out in the middle of nowhere, probably turned at least a couple of kids into budding evangelists.

The crowd scrambled to its feet and looked at Iggy as a beacon of hope. Which, considering the screwed-up mental place these kids were in, he was.

"Welcome back, Iggy. I was worried when your family kidnapped you," the kid who seemed to be leading this little séance said. I recognized him as Josh, the guy who'd given Dylan and me the flyers at Ella's school.

"They're buttheads," Iggy said, obviously having a little fun.

The rest of us were lurking in the shadows not far away. I made a face at Nudge, who clapped a hand over her mouth to keep from laughing.

"Iggy, you're the future of humankind," Josh went on. "You've adapted to the requirements of a harsher New World. We're the future too. Join us!"

The podkids gathered closer, Ella included, smiling and trying to touch Iggy.

"If Iggy's the future, I guess we're all going to need spray-on tans and sunglasses," I muttered to Total.

"I *am* the answer!" Iggy's voice boomed.

Total giggled. "That ham!" I poked him with my foot.

"He's the answer! He's the answer!" they chanted.

"Prove you cherish the One Light!" Iggy yelled, which I thought was a tad dramatic. "Do you want to be like the Igster?"

"Yes! Yes!" they said feverishly, and I shuddered, remembering how one of them had offered to gouge out his eyes back at the rally so he could be blind like Iggy.

Iggy crouched down and grabbed a handful of dusty dirt from the ground and spit into it. Then he walked over to Josh, who looked a little uncertain, and wrote his name on the guy's face with his finger. One by one the brainwashed kids spit into their dirty hands and smeared "IG" on their own cheeks. It was freaky. And kind of amazing.

"And...this is why Iggy's not the flock leader," I whispered to Nudge.

The kids all started flapping their arms and shrieking, and since they looked a bit distracted, Iggy pulled Ella over to the side, near where the rest of us were hiding.

"Iggy?" Ella said, turning to look at him. "How did you find us?"

"Um...my heart...led me here," Iggy said, thinking fast. "Now we just need to convince the rest of the flock to join the group. Gee, look—there they are!"

I took that as my cue and stepped out of the darkness toward Ella. She looked surprised to see me and even more surprised when Dylan sidled up next to her. But then her programming took over, and she needed to share the message with us.

"We must embrace the One Light." Ella beamed.

"The One Light?" I asked. "Oh, yeah, the One Light. Remind me of its glory."

"The One Light will show us how to become less and how to become more," Ella said with conviction.

"What the heck does that mean?" I whispered to Dylan.

"Like, they'll have genetic material stripped away and then replaced?" Dylan guessed quietly. I met his eyes and nodded, and then I remembered the last time I was out in the desert with him, at night. I turned away so he wouldn't see me blush.

"Right, right," said Iggy. "And when will this happen?"

"In five days," Ella told him. "When the Doomsday Group calls us home, all across the world. The world will end, but we'll go on living."

My eyes widened. Not good news.

"You got it, El," I said. "But first we're just going to take a detour for a little therapeutic deprogramming session."

"No," Ella's face darkened. "I want to stay here. Everyone needs to stay right here."

But Dylan moved in quickly, grabbing her under one arm. Iggy got a grip under the other. They flew off into the night, with Ella shrieking between them and the Doomsdayers wildly flapping their arms down below.

45

AFTER THE FIRST five minutes at the convention center hosting Comic-Con, Fang thought he'd seen it all:

- Attendees ranging from nine-year-old geeks to ninety-year-old scenesters in costumes featuring tentacles that moved, wings that moved (but were too small to actually support anyone's weight), and antennae that moved, and even a pair of blinking eyes in the back of one guy's head
- Short, short skirts on hundreds of girls dressed as anime characters, Haruhi, and Lara Croft, with complimentary, as Ratchet put it, "boob salad"
- Lots and lots of Trekkies

- People dressed up like him and Max and the rest of the flock
- People who wanted his autograph
- And, worst of all, birdkid manga based on the flock that, unfortunately, featured him and Max in several torrid embraces

"Hot," said Maya from behind him. Fang coughed and abruptly closed the Max manga.

But Maya just laughed. "Lead on," she said, taking his arm.

The main room was the size of several football fields, with a thirty-foot ceiling and high windows. Blue carpeting defined aisles that were lined on either side by booths. On the perimeter were huge, ornate displays for Lucasfilm and Marvel Comics, among others.

Fang felt trapped, claustrophobic, like he was on a wild goose chase before the chase had even started. But, oddly, having Maya on his arm sort of helped. It wasn't the kind of thing Max would have done. Maya wasn't quite as hard as Max, not quite as tough. She was different, and Fang kind of . . . liked it.

Fang's gang clustered near him as streams of people flowed through the big revolving doors at the front of the building.

"This is going to be awesome," Holden raved as a pair of girls dressed in skimpy anime costumes pushed past them.

There was barely room to move. A big lizard's long tail

whacked Fang's ankle, making him wince. Ratchet's green eyes almost popped out of his head as a buxom model dressed as Wonder Woman strode past, bracelets sparkling.

"How could the Doomsday Group hold a rally inside a huge, crowded building like this?" Fang asked. Even he could hear the lack of confidence in his voice. He'd read online that this year's convention expected more than one hundred thousand visitors over four days. All inside. Surrounding him. It was pretty much one of his top-five worst nightmares. What had he been thinking?

"Maybe they'll have a special table or a booth," Holden Squibb suggested.

More people swarmed past, most of them in costume. They saw sci-fi and fantasy characters, hundreds of comic book characters, old and new — people dressed up as virtually every kind of character, movie star, and species imaginable. But what hadn't they seen? You got it. Anything remotely related to the Doomsday Group.

Wait a minute! That's why the DG must be holding their rally here, Fang thought. Any kind of enhanced kid, any freak of nature, anything the least bit out of the ordinary wouldn't be noticed here. They'd blend in perfectly, and no one would bat an eye, or multiple eyes, as the case may be.

Kate and Star looked at each other nervously as four Stormtroopers thundered down the hall, brandishing weapons.

Every hair on the back of Fang's neck stood up when he realized that those weapons could be real. These people could all be spies. This whole thing could be a setup, a huge trap that he had walked right into. But this was the only lead he had.

"Oh, man…" Fang rubbed his chin. He looked at his gang—each member special, with amazing powers. But how were they at fighting? At escaping? Would it be the stupidest thing in the world to send them on their way, possibly putting them in danger?

"Okay, everyone, stay together," he instructed in a low voice. "Keep your eyes open for anything having to do with the DG. A T-shirt, a bumper sticker, anyone mentioning it, anything at all, you tell me. Got it?"

"Got it," said Star, as she saluted crisply.

Fang was starting to understand why he felt so freaked out. Here, among all these costumed people, he and Maya and the others were normal. They were average because everyone else was so extreme. Was that what the DG wanted? To enhance everyone, so everyone would be "special"?

But…if everyone was special, wouldn't that really mean that no one was special at all?

46

"MAYBE THE PEOPLE who said there'd be a rally here didn't know what they were talking about," Ratchet suggested when the gang got outside the convention center. "I was listening to everyone, everywhere, and I didn't—"

Suddenly he stopped dead in his tracks and held up a finger, adjusting his headphones. The others looked at him. He closed his eyes and very slowly turned his body slightly to the left. Fang waited, shrugging when Maya raised her eyebrows at him.

Ratchet opened his eyes. "It's that way," he said, pointing northwest.

Fang turned. There was another big building across the street. "Over there?"

Ratchet shook his head. "No. On a hill outside of town.

I just heard some people talking about it a mile from here. The rally will start at sunset." He grinned, confident in his skills, his dark face lighting up. "Superhearing."

"That's *so cool*," said Holden.

It *was* cool, Fang thought. Useful. But sad. He wondered how many other kids like Ratchet had been experimented on.

They arrived at the site just as the sun was setting. Hundreds of kids—*only* kids—were milling around a large outdoor arena. Older kids stood at the gates, ushering everyone inside.

"Welcome, friends," said a boy near the gate. "Thank you for coming. Thank you for being part of the solution."

"You're welcome," Holden said, as the gang entered.

Inside, a large stage was set up in the middle of the arena. The stadium seating went all the way up to the top. Fang and his crew grabbed seats in the front row, close to an exit.

A teenage girl appeared onstage, and everyone clapped. She held up her hand for quiet, and instantly all were silent.

"Thank you for coming," she said. Fang recognized her sweet, persuasive voice immediately.

"That's the girl from the news," Fang whispered to Maya. "The hypnotizing brainsucker."

The girl looked healthy and happy, mature for her age, and really pretty. "I hope you're all here for the Doomsday Group rally," she went on. "If you thought this was a Susie

Lee concert, you're in the wrong place." She smiled, and quiet laughter filled the stadium.

"So, who are we?" she said. "Well, my name is Beth, but that really doesn't matter. What matters is that I believe in the One Light."

All around Fang, kids leaned forward, nodding. Many repeated "the One Light, the One Light."

"For those of you who are new, you might be wondering what the One Light is," said Beth. The audience snickered, finding it hard to believe anyone would not know that. "Well, the One Light is...hope."

Spontaneous cheers broke out.

"This chick is cool," Ratchet said in Fang's direction.

Fang looked at him sharply. "Don't talk to anyone, and run if someone starts looking at you all crazy-eyed. Let me know if you suddenly feel...extra happy."

"Oh, like that's gonna happen," Star muttered.

Ratchet turned to her, then Fang nudged Star in the ribs and glared at Ratchet.

"Hey, man, I'm cool," said Ratchet. "I'm just saying it doesn't sound all that bad, you know?"

Onstage, Beth smiled and raised her hands. Behind her, on a massive screen, images scrolled: children running through a field of wildflowers; a deer drinking from a bucolic crystalline stream; golden wheat waving in the breeze; healthy, happy adults sitting around a big dining table, raising their glasses to the camera; a little girl holding a tiny lamb in her lap; a woman weaving cloth on a loom. It went on and on, one idyllic scene after another.

"What does the One Light teach us?" Beth asked. "It teaches us that we're responsible for ourselves and for our own actions. Right?"

The crowd murmured in agreement.

"The One Light is not about hatred," said Beth. "The One Light is about love—love for each other, love for our Earth Mother, love for the animals in our care."

The crowd shouted "Yes!"

Beth pointed a clicker at the screen, and a new series of images began. Now the pictures were of slash-and-burn farming, oil slicks, factories belching smoke, cities congested with traffic, nuclear power plants, thousands of chickens pressed together in crowded factory farms.

The audience groaned, upset by what they were seeing, and Fang noticed tears streaming down Kate's cheeks.

"This is exactly what I've been talking about!" Kate whispered to the gang. "That's where your Cluck-fil-A comes from!"

Still more disturbing images followed, of starving people, abandoned villages, trash-strewn lakes, and factories dumping pollutants into rivers.

With each new picture, the audience got a little bit louder, a little bit angrier.

"Um, I think Kate and Ratchet might be right. This doesn't seem that far-fetched to me," Maya said quietly.

"Something's still off—think of every DG member we've seen," Fang said.

"Who has done this to our Earth Mother?" Beth asked from the stage. "Was it me? No. Was it you?"

"No!" the audience shouted, shaking their heads.

"Is it enough for them to say they're sorry? That they didn't mean to do it? That they'll try not to let it happen again?"

"No!" the audience roared.

"That's right," Beth said with a smile. "People who do stuff like this never learn. They need to be prevented from doing it again and again. We need to wipe the slate clean and start over in a brand-new world. We're here to say, 'You've done enough harm, enough damage!'" Beth was pacing around the stage.

The audience repeated, "Enough!"

"We want a clean world, clean air, healthy food, healthy animals!" Beth declared.

"Yeah!" the audience yelled.

"These sick, hateful jerks," Maya said wryly, giving Fang a look.

"Something's off," he insisted.

"And all we need to do," Beth said with a smile, "is *kill* all the humans."

"Bingo," said Fang.

47

"STOP! STOP!" ELLA sputtered. "You're killing me! *Please!* Stop!" tears flowed down her cheeks as she shrieked and thrashed and tried to kick Dylan and Iggy.

I would never get used to this.

We didn't know whether the cold shower had made Iggy vulnerable during his deprogramming or if Angel had just gotten really good at mind hacking, but in the absence of a glacial stream in the middle of the desert, we figured that dousing Ella in a natural hot spring couldn't hurt. Dylan and Iggy were struggling to hang on to Ella's hands, and their faces were flushed and damp from the steam. I'd tested the water first—no reason to scald my half sister or cook her like an egg—and I knew it was pretty dang hot.

"How about now?" Iggy panted. "She's not made out of cotton balls, you know—my arm's tired."

"Hang on a sec," Angel said, looking worn-out herself. "I'm almost done."

Ella suddenly slumped into the water, all fight gone.

"Here she comes," I said, watching her.

Slowly Ella raised her head, blinking and shaking water from her face. I nodded to Dylan, and he and Iggy brought her over to the fire we'd built.

"What are you doing? Are you crazy?" Ella asked. She was sopping wet from head to foot, her long, dark hair plastered to her back. She wiped the water from her eyes and stared at me, confused. We continued to watch her.

She blinked and looked around. "Where are we?"

"Middle of the desert," I said, biting into an apple.

Ella blinked hard, studying each of our faces. "Iggy? What's . . . going on?"

"Sorry about the hot spring," he said, putting his arm around her. He eased her closer to the fire, then wrung water out of her hair. She looked disoriented and upset but definitely like herself. Iggy brought her up to speed.

"Where's Mom?" Ella finally asked, looking at me, and I took a deep breath. My eyes met Dylan's, and he stepped forward, kneeling in front of Ella.

"Your mom and Jeb left the house while Max and I were gone. They didn't tell anyone where they were going. They didn't take the car, and we can't find them."

Ella's eyes grew alarmed. "Were they kidnapped?"

"Maybe," Dylan said hesitantly. "Or maybe they're being influenced by the same thing that influenced you and the others." He spoke gently, slowly, giving Ella time to absorb what he was saying. I was...impressed.

Ella started crying, and I put my arm around her shoulders, mouthing "Thanks" to Dylan. And I meant it.

He gave me a smile, not quirky and crooked like Fang's, but open and sincere. And, weirdly, I felt my heart skip a beat.

"I'm so sorry, Ella" I said, rubbing her back. "I know it's hard. It's hard not knowing who to trust or where to turn. My life has been so weird that I pretty much expect to be betrayed, expect weird things to happen. But I know it's different for you."

"I can't believe it!" Ella sobbed. Iggy stroked her hair, which had started drying in the warmth of the fire.

"Listen," I said, "I was thinking. How about we take you to your aunt's place tomorrow after a good night's rest? I'm sure Tia Cita will let you hang out there till we figure out what's going on with Mom. We're going to find Mom and Jeb and get the real scoop. Maybe we'll be surprised. Maybe we'll need to rescue them. I'm not sure."

"No!" Ella said, her face still streaked with tears. "I'm going with you! I'm staying with you and Iggy!"

I shook my head. "I wish you could, but we're going to be flying. I promise we'll come back for you. Okay?"

Ella didn't look like it was okay, but she nodded yes

and wiped her eyes. We sat there together in the moon-
light, sharing food we had "acquired" from Ella's friends
back at the campfire. Almost everyone I cared about was
here, all in one place.

With a couple of major exceptions.

48

THE CROWD WAS so loud, Fang almost jumped. The kids were all on their feet now, and Fang motioned to the others to stand up. Reluctantly, Fang's gang joined the chant: "Save the planet! Kill the humans!"

"Whoa!" Holden said next to Fang, scanning the crowd. "When we got here, everyone looked weird and happy, but pretty normal, you know? Now look around."

Fang quickly studied the gathered assembly.

"Oh, my God," Maya said slowly. "Where did they come from?"

"I guess they must have been drawn in by the crowd," Fang replied. "They must have been hiding their...freakiness, at first. Kind of like you and I hide our wings sometimes."

"We're different, but we're okay," said Star. "But these guys…"

"What happened to them?" Kate asked. "The same thing that happened to us? Will we become like that?"

One of every ten kids in the audience was…genetically altered. Growing up in the School, trapped in their dog crates, Fang and the flock had seen lots of genetic combinations that didn't turn out as cute kids sporting big wings. And he was seeing it again, right here.

They weren't horrible disasters—they could breathe and walk and talk. Some of them even looked pretty human, except for, say, scaly skin or lizard eyes or claws for hands. But others were definitely freakish, and a bunch of them looked as though their combinations were not meshing entirely and breaking down.

"Will you join me in a song?" Beth asked over the frenzied roar. She stood center stage and began to sing. Gradually, the audience stopped chanting and began singing.

"I didn't know where I was going
I didn't know where I'd come from
But then one day I got the message
That I could save the world.
The One Light has shown me the way.
Because we're Gen 77
The skies will be blue, the seas will be green
But to get there, the blood must flow red.
We will become less, we will become more

We'll kill all the humans
And we'll save the world."

"Cheerful little ditty," Fang said. Maya nodded solemnly as she sang along. Then a noise overhead made Fang look up, in time to see thousands of colorful flyers dropping out of a helicopter. One floated close to him and he snatched it out of the air.

"The Enhanced People's Manifesto," he read.

All around him, the crowd began chanting: "Save the planet! Kill the humans! Save the planet! Kill the humans!"

Onstage, Beth beamed lovingly.

49

BACK AT THE hotel, Fang pored over the manifesto.

"I can't believe they're saying this stuff in black and white," Kate said, her eyes wide.

"Can't they be arrested for this?" Holden asked.

Fang frowned. "I don't know. They could say that it's just talk, not an actual threat. There's no evidence that they're really prepared to do any of it."

Maya waved the manifesto in the air. "Do we need more evidence than flyers saying they're going to kill everyone? It's all right here!"

Fang sighed. "I know."

The manifesto fit on the front of a single sheet of paper, but it was a doozy. It stated that the Doomsday Group planned to take over several countries, kill their populations, and then repopulate them with enhanced people, the so-called Seventy-seventh Generation.

It said that the apocalypse was coming—no news there—and offered tips about what to do when it hit.

It talked about a dark period of chaos and peril that would give way to a paradise in which all enhanced people would live together in peace and harmony.

"I'm so sure," Maya said. "Not unless everyone's going to be tranquilized forever."

"They just might be," Fang cautioned, and she frowned. "If they've managed to brainwash this many people, then who knows? They could easily tranquilize whole populations."

"Look at this," Star said, pointing. "They really do mean only enhanced people. It says here that people who fly shouldn't risk landing on top of tall buildings."

"'Those of you who might lay eggs,'" Kate read, "'will need to prepare a safe incubation container. Go to our website for sources.' Oh, my God. These people are crazy!"

"There were truckloads of those Gen 77 kids at the rally," Ratchet said. "I've never seen so many freaks in one place."

"Welcome to my world," Fang said. "Okay. We need more info. Like, when is all this supposed to happen, for instance?"

Maya rested her head on her hand. "Do you think Armageddon can wait till morning? I'm wiped."

Eyes closed, brown hair tousled around her shoulders,

Maya looked more like Max than ever. But...Fang could now see minuscule differences: the way Maya tilted her head, the way her voice dropped instead of rising at the end of a question. True, Max and Maya were much more alike than they were different, but Fang was starting to think of Maya as truly being a unique person in and of herself, instead of as just a copy of Max. It was weird. Fang had loved Max for so long that it almost disturbed him to think about any other girl at all.

He closed his eyes for a moment, feeling bone tired and confused. He'd thought taking out this Doomsday Group would be a good mission, a worthwhile project for him and his gang. And he was right. But after today, he had to admit an uncomfortable truth: As much as he'd wanted to operate on his own, this mission was way too big for him and five new crew members, only one of whom had any real fighting experience. Preventing the destruction of whole populations of people was simply beyond the scope of his gang.

That left him just one option.

Fang opened his bleary eyes, scanning the room until he found the clock. Past midnight. Getting yelled at by Max would have to wait until morning.

50

I WOKE UP, feeling warm on one side and cold on the other. The warm side rested against Dylan, and the cold side faced the open desert, which was aglow in pink from the sunrise.

I decided to get the fire started for the others. I untangled myself from Dylan, feeling the usual embarrassment and confusion that I often had about him. But I'm great at not thinking about mushy stuff, so I pushed it out of my mind and scooted over to the fire. Automatically, I did a head count, like I'd done just about every day for as long as I can remember.

Gazzy, Nudge, Dylan, Angel, Iggy, Total...Ella?

No Ella.

I jumped to my feet and surveyed the area. No Ella. Her

footsteps led away from us, but the desert wind was so efficient and the ground so hard and dry that her trail disappeared. I cursed under my breath.

"Max?" Angel said softly. "What's this?" She pointed to the ground, where words had been scratched into the hard dirt:

I was meant to have wings.
Ella

"We should have hobbled her," Total said, getting to his feet. "Or at least tied her shoelaces together."

Then it hit me.

"Oh, my God! She's going back to the facility!" I said. "Come on! If we hurry, maybe we'll reach her before she finds those kids again—or before she gets lost and ends up frying herself in the desert. Let's go!"

My team was mobilizing when my hip pocket vibrated. "This might be her!" I said, and flipped my phone open.

"Max?" said a voice, and my breath caught in my throat. "Don't hang up!"

Numbly, I brought the phone down from my ear and closed it. Then I sat on a rock, my blood so cold that it moved sluggishly through my veins.

Nudge said, "Max?"

Dylan came and sat next to me and put his hand on my knee. I pushed it off. My phone rang again, the dull vibration sounding like a buzz saw in the silence.

"Max? Who is it?" Nudge asked. "What's wrong?"

"My guess would be Fang," Dylan said, his voice flat.

I looked up to see Nudge's surprised face. Iggy, Angel, and Gazzy all looked at me sympathetically, like they expected me to wuss out.

My phone vibrated.

Gritting my teeth, I flipped it open.

"What," I said tightly.

"Don't hang up!" said Fang.

"In the middle of something here," I said. "Is this important?"

"Only if you consider the end of the world important," said Fang. "Which, I guess, usually you have."

I didn't say anything.

"Look, I'm in San Diego," Fang said. "I need you guys to come here."

My eyebrows shot up to my hairline. I still didn't say anything.

Fang sighed. "Max. I know you're mad. I know things are messed up between us. I know there's no reason in the world for you to trust me or to bother coming here. And believe me, I'm not trying to mess with you or make you feel worse. I'm not playing games. But I've stumbled onto something huge. Something very bad. And I think we have only days to stop it. I wish I could do it by myself, but I can't. I wish I didn't have to ask you for help, but I do. Come to San Diego. *Please.*"

His voice was like salt being rubbed into my wounded

heart. It literally made my pain worse. I couldn't believe he was doing this. I tried to swallow, but I felt like I had a big rock in my throat.

I didn't trust myself to speak. He was the only person in the world who could get to me this way. The only one. With horror, I felt that hot, prickly feeling behind my eyes that signaled tears were coming.

I'd cried more in the past year than I had in all fourteen years before. I was tired of crying. Tired of crying over Fang.

Dylan shifted impatiently in front of me. I looked up at his face and was surprised to realize that he felt a confusing mix of anger and hurt and caution. I had the power to hurt Dylan's feelings. And I felt like I had no power over Fang at all.

I swallowed. "Oh, yeah?" I said, and congratulated myself on how casual I sounded.

There was a pause. Fang was speechless. Good.

"Yes," he said finally. "Will you come? Will you bring the flock? I'm at the Crescent Bay Hotel, on Market Street, downtown. I can explain everything when you get here."

"We're pretty busy," I hedged.

"Max, the Doomsday Group has to be stopped!" Fang said forcefully.

I sat up straight, my jaw dropping. "The Doomsday Group?"

BOOK THREE

PARIS IS BURNING

51

THE FLOCK VOTED to go join Fang in San Diego rather than stay here to look for Ella. I did not exercise my executive veto. It made sense that we should try to cut off the head of the monster instead of attempting to rescue one small escaped mouse. But the thought of Ella going back to those weirdos, the thought of someone experimenting on her, or, worse, grafting wings on her, sickened me.

I cursed to myself the whole way to San Diego. We got there in the late afternoon. Fang had called again and said to meet him at the hotel restaurant. This news was met with loud cheers, since of course everyone was starving.

When we got there, I did something completely out of character: I stopped off at the ladies' room, yanked a brush through my snarls, washed my hands and face, and put on a relatively clean shirt from my backpack. When I came out, six pairs of eyes were staring at me like I'd turned into a porcupine.

"What?" I snapped defensively.

"You look fine," said Nudge, giving me a little smile.

"I have no idea what you're talking about," I said frostily.

I didn't know what I expected to see—I guess the same old Fang I'd always known, the one with the scruffy hair and dark clothes. The one with the crooked smile and midnight eyes. The one who'd broken my heart so, so badly.

I scanned the restaurant quickly, doing an automatic three-sixty, in case, I don't know, some Erasers or Flyboys or Dumb-bots hadn't gotten the memo that they'd been retired. Instead, I saw a tall, dark figure standing up, looking right at me. I clenched my teeth, tried to look expressionless, and led the flock over.

Then I saw that he wasn't alone. Four teenagers were sitting at his table, watching us alertly. These were probably members of the Fang Fan Club—

"Max," Fang said, reaching a hand out to me, then changing his mind and letting it drop to his side. "Thanks for coming." We looked into each other's eyes for a long minute, as if trying to peer into each other's brains, trying to read the subtext and the unspoken words. Then an irritated cough came from behind me, and Fang's eyes shot over to Dylan. A tiny, almost imperceptible wrinkle appeared between Fang's dark brows.

"Dylan," he said evenly. "I see you're still hanging around."

"Yep," Dylan said.

"Hey, guys," Fang said to the rest of them, his face softening. "Thanks for coming."

I felt the others hesitating, so I turned and forced a smile at Nudge and Angel. "It's okay," I said. "You can hug him, or whatever."

Then I plopped down in an empty chair and studied his new group, our replacements. There was a tiny, blond, cold-looking girl; a really pretty Asian girl with hair I'd kill for—and I'm not even that girly; a guy with headphones and some sweet sunglasses; and a scrawny kid who looked friendly, if a little beat up. Only one person was missing.

"Max," my voice said from behind me. I spun around only to see myself looking down at me with a slight sneer I knew all too well. "Gee, I haven't seen you since you tried to kill me," she said. Her smile was snarky, and I saw a couple of Fang's gang straighten in their seats.

The not-too-surprising thing was that Dylan was studying Max II, then me, while Fang glared at Dylan. Max II kept her eyes locked on mine.

This was going to be interesting.

52

IF BY "INTERESTING" I meant uncomfortable, awkward, infuriating, and horrible...then, yes, it was going to be most interesting.

I met Max II's eyes coolly. "I distinctly remember totally *not* trying to kill you."

I just couldn't believe it. I'd been so miserable since Fang had left, crying in the shower, crying up in trees, not sleeping, losing weight...so pathetic that they'd made me go to my mom's house—and in the meantime, Fang had quickly replaced us, gotten a haircut, and bought some new clothes. He looked perfectly fine. I clenched my fists under the table. Plus, he'd totally replaced me with *me*. It was so unfair.

"Anyway," I said. "Give me the scoop. And a menu."

Over the next half hour, Fang told us all the stuff they'd found out about the Doomsday Group, about the rally and Beth and the One Light. We told them about how DG fever was sweeping Arizona, how fast it was spreading. I also told him about seeing the weird computer guy out in the middle of the desert. Fang frowned.

"So basically, these people are talking mass destruction," said Dylan. "They've managed to alter who knows how many people" — he gestured to Fang's gang — "and to brainwash even more. But where did they come from?"

"We don't know," Fang said curtly, not looking at him. "That's what we've been saying."

I saw Dylan's jaw set. "Yeah? Is that what you've been saying? I must have missed that part. I thought you were still comparing pointless details."

Hey, wait a minute! Digging Fang was supposed to be my job...

"We're here to make a difference," Dylan continued. "So let's get to the point. The mission."

Fang's eyes flashed, and the energy that passed between him and Dylan could have made a hot dog sizzle. Gosh, guys are so cute, with that alpha male stuff. It's adorable!

"I agree," Max II jumped in, and somehow I felt like she was trespassing on my territory. "The question is, are we gonna join forces?"

"Yeah, Max," I said snidely. "That's a good idea. Put our two happy little families together. Then sit back and watch the fireworks."

She looked at me matter-of-factly. "My name isn't Max. It's Maya."

"Maya? You're kidding, right?" Now, I'm not saying I'm not usually obnoxious, 'cause, actually, I admit that I usually am. But I don't think I'm usually this obnoxious. At least, not to someone who wasn't a whitecoat or some other misguided, controlling grown-up.

Max/Maya blushed, and I could tell she was clenching her fists under the table. "Shut up," she said. "Who asked you?"

I stood up so fast my chair tipped backward. The other Max—I mean, Maya—stood up fast too. I was ready to punch someone's lights out.

"Catfight!" The guy wearing the shades snickered, and the icy blond girl elbowed him in the ribs, but she was smiling.

Dylan pushed back his chair, watching us carefully. Gazzy paused, his fork halfway to his mouth, as if gauging how many bites he could take before a battle broke out.

"Max," Fang said firmly, "we're not going to do this. Not here, not now."

Dylan frowned. "Don't tell her what to do! This is all your fault anyway!"

Fang looked at Dylan as angrily as I looked at Maya.

"Come on, Max," Fang said, throwing down his napkin. "Let's take this outside. You and me. It's time to settle this."

"Fine," I said, turning and stomping to the door. It was about time.

53

THE SMALL PARK next to the hotel was practically empty, and I quickly found a place to take off. I soared into the sky, my heart racing with adrenaline. I was so hyped-up and flooded with emotion that it felt fantastic to burn off some energy, heat dissipating through my wings. My strong primary and secondary feathers made effortless adjustments as I banked and turned, and within a minute I was a couple thousand feet up in the sky, in the wild blue yonder, as they say, where there was no sound except the wind rushing past my ears, nothing in my way, nothing holding me back.

I didn't even turn to see if Fang was following me. I figured he'd probably stayed behind with his new little wing-less gang. I was so angry and hurt and upset that I didn't know what to say to him. We'd had arguments before, of course, and knockdown, drag-out fights, but not too much recently. Not since we'd —

"So what's the deal?" came Fang's cross voice behind me.

I did a fast spin-brake, wheeled around, and faced him as we each rose up and down with the beat of our wings.

"You're asking me?" I said, incredulous. "I thought you were running everything! You decided to leave. You decided I should come back. You decided that we should have this out. I'm just your audience!"

"You've never been an audience!" Fang snapped. "You know I did the right thing by leaving—you're just too bullheaded to admit it! You know we need to work together to fight the Doomsday Group, but you'd rather flit around with your hurt feelings! And you *know* that you should have left Dylan behind in Arizona, but you'd rather throw him in my face!"

I was so stunned I couldn't think straight. I so did not agree that Fang had done the right thing by leaving. I don't believe that I've ever flitted anywhere in my life. And how was I supposed to leave Dylan anywhere? I didn't control him, and he seemed to have a homing device locked on me anyway.

I finally closed my mouth before I started swallowing bugs. "Throw him in your face? He's stuck to me like glue! How could I not bring him with me? Besides, you're the one posting cutesy videos of you and my stand-in online! How is that not throwing her in *my* face?"

"She's not your stand-in!" Fang roared. "She's a unique individual! It's not her fault that she looks like you!"

In my whole life, I couldn't remember being more furious with anyone who wasn't a total enemy. I was practically spitting. "Well, it's not my fault that Dylan imprinted on me! And you know what? He's the only one who hasn't left me! Why would I give that up?"

Fang's face blanched, and even I was shocked at what I'd said. We simply stared at each other, rising and falling, the air currents lifting us like waves in the ocean.

Fang was breathing hard, his teeth clenched so tight that even his lips were white. I was so upset and pumped with adrenaline that I felt like I might throw up. Such a bummer that would be for anyone below me...

I don't even know how long it was before Fang swallowed, coughed, and then said, "The Doomsday Group is bigger than this, bigger than us. Do you agree that we should both try to fight it?" His voice was a little ragged now but calmer.

I took several deep breaths. "It would probably be best if we both fought it," I said stiffly.

Fang nodded, some of the color returning to his face. "Please tell Dylan to go back to Arizona. This isn't a fight for newbies."

And just like that, I was furious again. "Newbies!" I exclaimed. "Like your little team of high-schoolers down there? They can't even freaking fly! At least Dylan can kick butt in battle! I'd trust him with my back before I'd trust any of the kids in the Fang Show!"

Fang opened his mouth to yell back but stopped himself with effort. "Maya is a good fighter," he said finally.

"Yes, I am," I said sharply.

Again his eyes blazed and his mouth opened, but again he controlled himself. He let out a deep breath. "She's not you," he said quietly. "She really is a different person."

I crossed my arms over my chest. "I'm not asking Dylan to go."

Fang's fists clenched. "We need Maya on our side."

Minutes of silence. If we hadn't been two thousand feet in the air, we would have heard crickets chirping. I stared at him as if we were strangers, brown eyes looking into black.

"So . . . where does that leave us?" Fang said.

"It leaves us with Dylan and Maya, all of us fighting the DG together," I said. "As revolting as that sounds."

Fang nodded stiffly and held out one hand.

I almost snorted but reached out and shook it. We had an agreement.

And as we flew back down to the restaurant, all I could think was, *What happened to us?*

54

I WAS SWEATY and my hair tangled in knots by the time we walked back into the restaurant. So much for tidying up for this meeting! As we approached the table, I saw that our two groups seemed very...separate. No one was talking. They watched each other warily.

When I got closer, I heard Gazzy say, apropos of nothing, "We can fly."

"So can we," said Maya, eyeing Fang. "Well, some of us."

"I can see really, really far," said Dylan, not missing a chance to outdo Fang.

"Me too," said the tough-looking guy, adjusting his Ray-Bans. "I can hear really far too. Whispers from a mile away and all."

"Well, we can breathe underwater," Angel offered,

modestly avoiding any mention of the fact that she can also read minds.

"So can I," said the pale kid. "I can regenerate and heal really fast."

"We heal fast too," Iggy countered. "And we're really strong."

"Try me," said the pretty Asian girl. "Let's arm wrestle."

"Um, I can hack most computers," Nudge said mildly.

"I'm fast enough to steal any computer we'd need," said the blonde.

Gazzy didn't miss a beat and said, "Fast enough to dodge *this?*" then sent a forkful of mashed potatoes flying through the air. Fast Girl dodged it easily, but then Gazzy snapped his fork to the left, flinging a glob right at...wait for it...Maya. And it hit her in the face. I couldn't believe my eyes.

"Oops," Gazzy said with a nervous grin. "My bad."

Maya wiped off her cheek and stood up, flashing a look that could kill. She grabbed the basket of rolls and began pelting Gazzy with them, lightning fast.

Gazzy laughed and ducked, taking no offense. "Food fight!" he cried happily.

Immediately, the uncivilized hellions in my flock and the free-wheeling punks in Fang's gang let all their inhibitions go. Nudge tossed her milk shake at the blond girl. The scrawny kid mashed his hamburger in Iggy's face. It fell to the floor, and Total dropped on it like a small, black avenging angel. Angel methodically dipped fries in ketchup and launched them at anyone she could. Fang and I were waving our arms and shouting for them to stop, but they were well beyond hearing us. Out of the corner of my eye, I saw some security guards starting to make their way over to our table. Just like old times.

And then it hit me: things had actually been fairly peaceful with Fang and me apart. Horrible and heart-breaking but quiet. Now that we were in the same room, all heck was breaking loose. Maybe we *were* better off apart? Maybe the whole freaking world was better when we were apart?

"Guys!" I shouted. I was about to tell my flock to do an up-and-away before we all got arrested, and then, all of a sudden, Dylan jumped up on a chair.

And he started to sing.

55

I'D SEEN THE effect of Dylan's singing before. It would stop a rabid dog in its tracks. And it had the same effect now.

"When I look in your eyes, I see the ocean," he sang, and the food fight started moving in slow motion.

"When I look in your heart, I see myself.
When we're apart, I'm just a shadow.
Can't you see, oh can't you see,
We were meant to be..."

Glancing around quickly, I saw that the kids had stopped, freezing in position as if they were playing statue.

The security guards had stopped too, and were standing still, listening to Dylan, mesmerized by his beautiful voice. The diners who had been fleeing the chaos paused and turned around. Then Dylan locked his eyes on mine.

"You and me, we're a team," he crooned.

"You and me, we're a dream...
Is this real? Are you what you seem?
I can tell you, you can count on me.
Can't you see, oh can't you see,
We were meant to be..."

I can't describe the effect his voice had on me—it was like soothing honey, calming my nerves. And it wasn't just me—people were clapping, the food fight was forgotten, the security guards were beaming as if they expected Dylan to whip out an engagement ring and pop the question.

The only person decidedly *not* mesmerized and charmed was...Fang. He watched Dylan solemnly, not angry, not tense. But definitely not like honey had just dripped all over his heart.

Dylan reached down, took a rosebud from the vase on the table, held it out to me, and smiled. His stunningly good looks made me weak.

"Let's get out of here," he said.

I couldn't even speak. I took the rosebud and made my

way carefully through the tables out of the restaurant, while behind us people clapped. I didn't even glance back to see if anyone was coming with us.

Dylan pushed through the revolving door, then we were out in the balmy San Diego air. I turned to him.

"Thank—" I began to say, but he gently put his hand on my neck, bent down, and kissed me, smothering my words.

"I'm here for you," he said intently, looking into my eyes.

And I couldn't speak.

56

I RESTED MY head drowsily against a soft pillow, feeling the muffled roar of the jet's engines. In just a few short hours, so much had come together: Fang had figured out that the Doomsday Group's headquarters were in Paris— one of my favorite cities. We'd called on our benevolent sponsor, Nino Pierpont, who just happened to be one of the richest men in the world, and now we were in one of his many private jets, heading to Europe. My flock could fly fast but not as fast as a jet. Besides, few of Fang's gang could fly, even though Star could run really fast.

I'd picked a seat in a corner, grabbed a blanket and pillow, and curled up, exhausted, only half listening to the murmur of voices in the background. The flock and Fang's gang were—right now, at least—tentatively getting along.

But that definitely wouldn't last—Gazzy had suggested a game of poker.

"Yeah, and so Max and Dylan are supposed to, like, go to Germany and have kids together," I heard Gazzy say.

My eyes popped open and I bolted upright.

"*What?*" Fang said, his voice icy.

"Gazzy!" I yelled.

Wide blue eyes looked at me in surprise, then back at Fang's stoic face. "Oh. Was I not supposed to say anything?" Gazzy asked.

"What is he talking about?" Fang demanded, glaring at me, then Dylan.

"Nothing. Just some crazy stuff that Dr. Hans came up with, in some hallucination," I said, squinting at Gazzy.

"Go off and have kids?" Fang demanded. I saw Maya watching him, her eyes studying his face.

"Yeah," said Dylan casually, fanning the flames.

"Oh, please," I said. "I can't even keep a goldfish alive."

"You and Dylan?" Fang said with an expression I'd never seen before. "Having kids?"

Fang's face never gives anything away. I'd seen him scared, furious, amused, impatient, and it all kind of looks the same. But this was different. I'd never seen him look this upset. Call me selfish, but it was kind of a relief that he could still get so upset over me, you know?

"Don't look at me—it was Hans's idea," I protested.

Dylan looked cool as a sea breeze. He stretched out his arms, then loudly cracked his knuckles. The butthead.

Fang almost had smoke coming out of his ears.

"You didn't think to mention this to me?" he asked me coldly.

My eyes narrowed, and when I spoke, the temperature inside the plane dropped several degrees. "When was I supposed to tell you?" I asked, deceptively calm. "When you told me not to look for you? When you told me not to contact you? When you told me to forget about you?"

There haven't been many times when I've rendered Fang speechless, so they're extra sweet when they happen. I enjoyed this one a lot. I mean, *a lot*.

Fang ran his hand through his somewhat shorter black hair and looked like he wanted to punch a hole in something.

I took a split-second to look around and realized that everyone was sitting silently, their eyes big, watching us as if we were a mongoose and a cobra.

And you know what? I hated that Fang and I were acting this way, hated that they had seen us fighting.

"I told you she was bad news," Maya said, breaking the silence. And that was when the cow pies really hit the fan.

57

I LOST EVERY bit of cool I had and turned angrily to Maya. "You stay out of this!" I snapped.

She leaped to her feet, knees flexed, hands like knife blades, karate-style.

"Who's gonna make me? You're just mad that Fang doesn't need you anymore!" Maya said, and I felt my blood boil.

"Yeah?" I snarled. "Is that why he replaced me with me?"

Her eyes flashed as she took a step toward me. To tell you the truth, pounding the heck out of someone right then would have been a relief. I was full of feelings that had nowhere to go, so knocking Maya's lights out would have felt pretty good.

Suddenly there was a little whoosh, and I got knocked

back a couple feet. The same invisible force threw Maya back, and we stood there blinking, wondering what had just happened. Then that girl Star appeared again, sitting down in her chair.

"You guys stop it," she said, as her hair settled into place. "I know twin sisters always fight, but you shouldn't. I would love to have a sister."

"We're not tw—" Maya and I both said, then stopped and looked at each other, frowning. We probably weren't twin sisters, but we didn't really know for sure. We might be. Or maybe she was just my clone. Actually, what's the difference? I needed to do a little research.

"I can tell all of you are mad at each other," Angel said, stepping to the middle of the aisle. "But I don't know why." She looked at all of us. "Is this what you want to do right now? I mean, Max and Fang each have their own flocks. Fang, you chose to leave, so you can't really argue with anything Max is doing now. If you wanted to have an opinion about it, you should have said something before you left."

I was surprised to hear Angel say that, and Fang looked stunned.

"She doesn't have to—" Fang started, but Angel held up her hand, with a stern, no-nonsense look that only a seven-year-old could pull off.

"Max can do what she wants," Angel said. "You can either stay and weigh in, or you can leave and have no say. That's how it works."

Fang opened his mouth, then closed it, looking like he

rued the day Angel learned to speak. He threw himself down in a chair, not looking at her, waves of heated anger almost visible.

I was in shock too. Angel had said things that I had felt but had been unable to put into words. She was summing up everything that was making me mad and expressing it so much better than I could have. I hadn't gotten much further than "Me mad."

"And Max," Angel said, turning to me, "you're the flock leader. Frankly, you need to do better than this."

I blinked.

"You're the flock leader when Fang is there, and you're the flock leader when Fang is gone. I know you'll always love Fang, but you shouldn't let him — or Maya — get to you like this. And you shouldn't let Dylan's feelings toss you around like a little boat without a sail. You're a big boat, Max. You have to act like it."

"I'm a...big boat?" I asked. She'd lost me back at "Maya."

"Yes," she said patiently. "You are. You're the leader, but you're acting like everyone else's feelings are more important than your own. Your feelings should be the most important feelings to you."

"I have to think about what other people feel," I protested. Especially since I'd been criticized in the past for not caring about other people's feelings!

"Yes," Angel agreed. "When it's a group decision or something that affects all of us. But you don't when it's something that's just about you. *You* decide how you feel about

Fang. *You* decide how you feel about Dylan. Quit letting everything else get in the way."

I started to wonder if Angel had been injected with some fancy experimental DNA-type thing that made her sound forty years older than she actually was. And honestly, her face seemed to have lost some of its baby roundness, I noticed, as if in a dream. Her words swirled all around me, like little rays of light clearing paths through my brain.

"Be with one or the other or neither of them," Angel concluded. "But just do it and quit whining about it."

I almost said something, then changed my mind. I am not a whiner. I have taken quite a lot without whining. But maybe Angel had a point.

Maybe she had a lot of points.

"The Japanese have an idiom for whining that is translated as 'vomiting up weakness,'" Total said helpfully.

I sat quietly for several moments, thinking, letting my mind sift through the confusion in my brain. When I finally spoke, I felt rock solid for the first time in weeks.

"We all need to fight the Doomsday Group," I said. "So we need to coordinate our efforts. But, for the most part, it seems to be bad news when Fang and I get together. So the groups should split up, each doing our own thing. But first we'll make a joint plan. Then we'll carry out our separate parts." I looked around. Nudge was nodding, Total was trying to give me a high four, and Fang gave a subtle nod: he agreed.

Dang, growing up was tough.

58

"STEP RIGHT UP and see the amazing superkids!" Fang shouted to the passersby as he shook a tambourine.

Behind him, Kate was juggling a cinder block, a locked safe, and a marble statue.

"Find something too heavy for her to lift!" Fang called. "She'll juggle anything you bring over!"

Fang had spent the first fourteen and a half years of his existence trying hard not to stand out. He'd developed a habit of extreme stillness that allowed him to blend in with whatever his surroundings were.

So this was not coming naturally to him.

Ratchet was listening in on people's conversations from ten yards away, then offering to "read their minds" when they came to check out the hubbub.

Star was racing around and sneaking up behind people, catching them unawares. They rubbed their eyes in disbelief.

And Holden? The fast-healing boy was breathing fire. He'd been practicing for almost an hour now and was doing pretty well, having set only two trees ablaze by accident.

"Fang! Check this out!" He took a swig of the flammable liquid and started burping his ABCs—in flame. "Ayyy, Beee, Ceee," he belched, fire shooting out of his mouth.

A crowd started to form where Fang's gang was putting on their show, not far from the amazing glass pyramid in the courtyard of one of the world's most famous museums, the Louvre. As soon as they'd all landed at Paris-Orly airport, Max and the flock had taken off to carry out their part of the plan. Fang's objective was to bait whatever DG scouts lurked throughout the city. They'd peopled their rally with Gen 77 kids and were probably on the lookout for more. So Fang and his crew were out in public, being as obviously Gen 77 as they could be.

Fang and Maya held hands, ran about twenty feet across the plaza, and launched themselves into the air. They spread their wings wide as people gasped and started taking pictures. While Ratchet and Holden passed the hat down below, Fang and Maya did acrobatic maneuvers, loop-de-loops, somersaults, steep dives, and whatever else they could think of.

By the time they landed, a crowd of at least a hundred

people had gathered, taking photos, clapping, and talking excitedly.

"We'll be here all week!" Fang said, passing the hat. He was amazed at how many people were tossing in euros. They might be able to quit stealing all the time. "*Merci!* Thank you! *Merci!*" said Fang, bowing. When he straightened up, a girl about his age stood there smiling at him.

"That was quite a show," she said in English.

"Thanks," said Fang.

"I'd like to invite you and your friends to another kind of show," she said, "the day after tomorrow. At the Place de la Concorde. Do you know it?"

"I'm sure we can find it," said Fang.

"Excellent," said the girl. "Here's a flyer. See you then!"

"Okay, see you then," said Fang.

After she walked off, he and the gang read the flyer. "Yes!" Fang said. "We did it!"

Let the One Light make your dark days disappear! Join us at the Place de la Concorde and experience the love and acceptance of the One Light. Be part of the solution! We're going to save the planet! Rejoice!

With love, from your friends at the Doomsday Group

59

"WHY ARE WE HERE?" I asked. "Typically, we don't do very well in places like this."

For some reason, we were meeting Fang and his gang at a fabulous restaurant in a superfabulous hotel—the Georges Cinq. It was decked out in a beautiful, opulent, unbirdkid-friendly, gray and gold interior. We usually tear up places like this, which is why I had lobbied for the McBurger on a little side street.

Fang nodded. "I know, but this is everyone's first visit to Paris. Possibly their last. I wanted to show them something special. Plus we found something that I think—"

"Actually we found something," I interrupted. "Something major. But let's get settled first." I hated how I was acting, trying to one-up him. We didn't actually have anything real. We'd just overheard something that we couldn't figure out.

The maître d' must have been used to rock stars and child actors and other reprobate types, because he didn't bat an eye as he led us to a long banquet table in an isolated corner. The thirteen of us sat down, all on our best behavior. Total, of course, was thrilled to pieces to be back in Paris, one of the few places on earth so civilized that dogs are allowed in stores and restaurants.

"Oh, my God. I can already smell the vichyssoise," he rejoiced, inhaling deeply.

"The what?" Gazzy asked, peering at the menu. "Um, this is all in French. I want a burger."

"Try the *boeuf haché*,'" Maya recommended, and I remembered Angel telling me that Maya had lived mainly in Europe since she'd been liberated from her cage in New York.

"So, what've you got?" Fang asked me while we waited for them to bring our drinks.

"Hm?" I asked, keenly aware that Maya was looking at me expectantly. Dylan raised an eyebrow, ready to come to my aid if necessary. "Oh, it's nothing." I coughed. "Just…we kept hearing all this stuff about D-day—like, the world ends day, we think—but people were pretty tight-lipped about it, so we don't know when this whole shebang is going down."

"Plus, we got a smidge caught up in sightseeing around ol' Paree," Total said, oblivious to my sharp glance. "Twelve patisseries, three parks, and four museums." He put his paws on the table and drank some water from a glass.

"Really," said Fang.

I paused, trying to frame our activities in a positive light. "We just went to as many places as possible where people might meet, where kids might want to go..."

"It may have been thirteen patisseries," Dylan added unhelpfully. "But we also hit a lot of schools. We saw at least two DGers hanging out at schools, scoping out the students."

"Checking the schools was my idea, since they seem most interested in kids," said Gazzy, helping himself to more bread and butter. In France, plain old bread and butter were just about the best things on earth. "The patisseries were Max's idea."

"Of course," said Fang, but I didn't react.

"Dude, quit playing with her," Ratchet said. "Are you gonna tell them what we found or not?"

Fang cocked an eyebrow at me, and I scowled.

Maya took a flyer out of her pocket and unfolded it so we could read it. "Yeah, we actually already knew about the D-day thing," she said. "But we got the inside info."

Fang smirked, and I kind of wanted to punch him.

Instead, I tried to act mature while reading the flyer, calmly seething. "Day after tomorrow," I said, shocked. "That's...soon."

We were all solemn as we pondered that thought. Until Gazzy broke the silence with, "No *duh*."

"We'd better make plans..." Fang began, but he didn't get very far.

Boom!

60

BOOM! THE WHOLE restaurant was suddenly rocked by a huge explosion that seemed to come from right beneath our feet. People screamed, the lights went out, and we heard glass breaking and walls crashing down.

"Stay together, everyone!" I yelled. "Let's get out of here!"

Carefully, we began to edge past hysterical people, relying on Iggy's extraordinary sense of direction, since most of us couldn't see anything through the smoke.

Le Cinq had a big freaking hole in its outside wall, and we made for it. I pulled my shirt up over my nose and mouth and kept hold of Nudge's arm. I also held onto Angel's hand as she yelled, "Calm down! Follow us! We'll get you out! No pushing!"

People around us were panicking, climbing over tables,

screaming. But I heard one unmistakable voice above it all: "*Max!*"

In an instant, I felt his breath on my neck, his hands on my shoulders. "I'm okay, Dylan," I called. "Get a grip." I found myself shrugging off his touch. *At least he gives a crap,* I thought. Unlike someone else, who was, mind you, out of sight.

Together we climbed over the rubble and through the hole, into the street. Sirens were already wailing. I quickly counted heads and felt a weird twinge when I saw Fang doing the same. All of us were safe.

Gazzy sniffed the air. "That's explosives. It smells like Christmas!"

Okay, so we've had somewhat untraditional Christmases. With explosives.

Suddenly, there was another explosion from deep within the building. The blast made us stagger, even from across the street. Down the block, the hotel's front doors opened and people poured out, panicked and screaming.

"We'd better move back," Dylan said. "The whole building's going to collapse."

"*Au secours!*" a voice wailed.

"That means 'help,'" Nudge said, looking around quickly. "Over there!"

Thirty feet away, a woman was pinned beneath a large chunk of building. I tried to lift the huge piece of rubble but couldn't budge it. Kate, one of Fang's gang, the girl who looked like a supermodel, hurried over.

"We need a crane or something!" I told her.

"No . . ." Kate bent her knees and placed her hands carefully to get a good grip on the boulder. I tried not to roll my eyes—at least she was making an effort.

In the background I heard another scream, a woman's voice, yelling for help too, but we could only do one thing at a time.

"We really need something big—" I began, then stared as she easily shifted the enormous piece of debris. She didn't even grunt or anything.

"Max!" Nudge yelled, then ran over.

"Help me!" I told her, and she and I carefully moved the woman out from under the rubble.

"That was *amazing!*" I told Kate.

"Max—" Nudge began.

Kate shrugged and blushed. "DNA splicing will do that for you," she said.

"Yeah, no kidding." I was still looking at her in awe.

"Max!" Nudge broke in again. "Angel's in the hotel!"

61

"NO SHE ISN'T," I said. "She came out with us!"

Nudge shook her head. "She's trying to save someone—she flew up to the top floor and went inside!"

"*Mon fils!*" a woman cried nearby, pointing.

I gaped at Nudge, my mind reeling as she pulled me toward the hotel. Nudge pointed to the spot Gazzy was staring at: there, on the top floor of the hotel, a small boy was leaning out an open window. One window over, flames were lapping out, eating the expensive silk curtains. The boy was crying and shouting for his *maman,* reaching for her.

"*Aidez mon fils!*" the woman screamed, pointing.

"Angel!" Gazzy cried.

Maya and Fang were already up there, hovering outside

the window. Angel was in the room with the boy, but he was terrified and wouldn't listen to her. She kept gesturing to the window, but he wouldn't budge.

"Why doesn't she just control his mind?" Gazzy asked, watching fretfully.

"The kid might be too upset," I said, not taking my eyes off Angel.

The little boy looked about four. I watched Angel talking to him earnestly. Then I saw flames enter the room and whoosh across the ceiling.

"Get out of there!" I shrieked.

Fang and Maya were beckoning to Angel and holding out their arms. A fire truck rounded the corner just then, sirens blaring, lights flashing.

Now the fire was very close to Angel and the boy. He was sobbing. On the street, his mother was wailing and wringing her hands. Then a billowing cloud of thick smoke rolled through the room, hiding the boy and Angel from us.

My mouth gaped in horror as I shot out my wings and started flying toward the window.

Fang and Maya were coughing from the smoke.

Suddenly, two figures jumped from the window.

"Angel!" I yelled.

Her once-white wings were dull and gray. The boy's weight was making her sag as she flew, but she held him tightly. They were both gasping for breath and coughing.

Fang and Maya went closer. Angel looked at them and

nodded. With one forceful stroke of her wings, she shot away from the building—just as the room exploded in flames, showering the sidewalk below with glass and debris.

I flew along the sidewalk beneath her, and with Fang and Maya flanking her on either side, Angel landed well down the block, setting the boy down gently. His mother raced up, shrieking in French, and grabbed him. He was coughing and sniffling but managed a smile as he motioned to Angel. The woman tearfully thanked Angel, who nodded wearily and then headed over to me. I met her halfway.

"Way to go, hero," I said, giving her a high five.

"Thanks." She smiled, her teeth bright white against her soot-covered face. "I bet you were dying to come get me."

I laughed ruefully. "You know me too well. I was going crazy."

Angel smiled again and took my hand. It was like old times.

62

I BASKED IN nostalgia for about a minute and a half, then my reverie vanished.

I saw Fang gathering up his gang. Maya said something that made him smile. He grinned back at her, and—right in the very same city that I myself was currently in—he pushed her hair away from her face. Just like he had done for me so many times.

I lost my breath, like I was getting punched in the stomach. It almost felt like my own personal D-day, where I was experiencing the end of "Fang and Max," forever.

Suddenly, I needed to get away. I told Nudge and Angel that I'd be right back and gave them a lame, totally unconvincing smile. Then I ran down the sidewalk and launched myself into the air, ascending as fast as I could. I soared over the city and followed the Champs-Élysées, the main boulevard, to the Arc de Triomphe, the center of twelve streets that radiate away from it.

I circled the city several times, high enough not to be seen but low enough to take in some of the sights—the Eiffel Tower, of course, Notre Dame, and Sacré-Coeur, high on its hill. A light drizzle began to fall, adding to my sadness. Streetlights came on, and the city twinkled.

Finally, I alighted atop the Arc de Triomphe. No one was up on the observation deck; I had it all to myself. The day had grown chilly, and I was damp all over, strands of hair plastered to my face. From up here, nearly two hundred feet in the air, I could see most of the city. It was amazingly beautiful.

I sighed, resting my head against one of the big iron spikes at the perimeter of of the Arc's deck.

I thought that I'd never see Fang again, but here we were, in Paris. At first I thought we'd always be together, but no. Then I thought we'd always be apart, but no again. I couldn't count on anything; I couldn't get used to either situation, because both kept changing. It was so frustrating! And so *unfair!*

I thought about what Angel had said, that I had to put my own feelings first when it came to Fang and Dylan. That would be easier if I actually knew what my feelings were. I wasn't sure I wanted to spend more time getting wet and chilly up here trying—and probably failing—to figure them out.

I sighed again. *I should go back,* I thought. *The flock will be wondering—*

Then a hand touched my shoulder. I spun around, muscles tense. It took a second for me to process Dylan's face, his unfolded wings, his look of concern.

"Don't sneak up," I said, feeling my heart pounding.

He gave a little smile. "At least I was able to. Ten points for me—I'm getting better."

"Didn't know we were keeping score," I mumbled. I turned away from him and looked out over the city as the sky got darker. "Everyone okay?" I asked, not looking at him.

"Some of Angel's feathers are singed, and her face is a little pink, but she'll be fine. Everyone else is okay. We got a suite in the same hotel Fang is staying at. But on a different floor."

"Great," I said, trying not to sound sarcastic. Dylan was quiet then, standing near me. Finally, I broke the awkward silence. "Is that why you're here? To let me know what hotel we're at?"

He frowned slightly, and I saw tiny drops of water on his face from the mist. "Not exactly. I came after you because you looked upset. And I wanted to be with you."

Again with the disarming honesty. The heart on the sleeve. I looked into his turquoise eyes and saw emotion there. Fang's eyes were so dark I couldn't see the pupils. And besides that, there was always layer upon layer of mystery, with Fang. Dylan's eyes were clear and open and full of...well, I couldn't let myself think it.

Dylan had come after me. Not Fang. But that wasn't reason enough to let him...in.

"About that being-with-me thing," I asked. "Why *is* that, really? Because if there's a little bot gene inside of you that says '*Me want Max*' all day long, I'm telling you right now, that's just gross. I'm not interested."

He watched me intently, and I wasn't sure if I felt like prey or predator.

"See?" I jumped in. "Time's up. You have no idea why you like me."

Dylan smiled and reached out, gently taking my hand. "Well, for starters...you're kind of beautiful."

Okay, I wasn't expecting that. Saving the world doesn't give you a whole lot of time to look in the mirror. I'd done it maybe half a dozen times at most in the past year, most of the time to wipe blood off my face and check out injuries.

He couldn't be serious.

"You have no idea how dumb that sounds, Dylan." I snorted and pulled my hand away. "I guess you're too *adolescent* to understand that girls want you to like them for who they are, not how they look."

Dylan shrugged. "I said 'for starters.' You didn't let me finish."

"So...be my guest." I tapped my fingers playfully on the railing as his eyes bored more deeply into mine.

"Waiting…" I said in a singsongy, now slightly jittery voice. He was moving toward me slowly, as if giving me a chance to protest. I didn't.

"Can we…talk about that later?" he asked. "I'm kind of…distracted right now."

But he couldn't have been more focused.

I didn't move—my back was against the safety bars. He touched my cold cheek with one hand, then pushed my damp hair away from my face. He ran his fingers down my tangly mop as if it were a strand of pearls.

When he looked back into my eyes, his expression gave me a little jolt.

"Um…" I said.

Then he stepped even closer and tilted his head slightly to one side, his eyes still locked on mine. I was frozen in place as his mouth touched mine and he kissed me. He was strong and warm and solid, and he gathered me to him, an arm around my waist. I didn't remember making a decision, but my arms found their way around his neck as he kissed me harder, holding me close in the mist.

And for a long time, it was just the two of us, silhouetted against the Paris skyline, the night deepening around us.

And it felt…right.

And kind of beautiful.

63

I AM NOT Miss Savvy about romantic relationships. The only one I've ever really had was with Fang, and, I admit, it was kind of strange to fall in love with someone I had grown up with. So I was quietly freaked out about kissing Dylan. Eventually, it dawned on us that we were really hungry, so we'd flown back to the hotel together, only to find everyone walking down the street to a little crepe place on the corner.

I'd felt Fang's sharp gaze studying our faces as we sat down, Dylan's leg warm against mine, and I started to feel self-conscious. Then I remembered what Angel had said: he could stay and weigh in, or leave and keep his mouth shut. That made me sit up straighter, and I smiled at Angel as I asked her to pass the bread. I didn't know what all this meant, didn't know where it was going, but for the time being, at least I wasn't running away screaming. Which was progress.

After dinner (which was fabulous—ham and cheese and potato crepe), we all walked back to the hotel together. Angel and I fell behind and were talking quietly while the others went ahead. I was half paying attention to what she was saying and half reliving kissing Dylan.

And I'm sure you already realize what I didn't remember till it was too late: Angel can read minds. And she isn't too particular about who's mind it is or when she reads it.

She took my hand. I looked down at her and saw that she had grown three inches, like, in the past couple months. "I'm sorry this is so hard, Max," she said. "I know it's all confusing.

"And I know how much you love Fang," she said, surprising me. "But that just doesn't seem possible anymore, you know?"

I made some sort of strangled noise—I was getting relationship advice from a seven-year-old. Because she knew more than I did. A new low.

"Max, we know how much you've done for us," she continued, my mind reeling. "You've made so many sacrifices for us, risked your life so many times. In a way, letting Dylan love you is another sacrifice—one you would make not just for us but for the future of the whole world."

Okay, now I was seriously wigging out. Was Angel saying I should flit off to Germany and have eggs with Dylan? I mean, WTH?

"And," Angel said, pausing before we went into the hotel, "it's a sacrifice that you could even be happy with, someday. Dylan is a great guy. And if he really was made for you, it'll make everything so much easier. He truly cares about you. If you let him in just a little bit, he could easily love you."

I felt like I was going to faint or throw up—that's what talking about emotions does to me—but I looked down into her big blue eyes. She gave me a little smile.

"I wish I could help, Max. I wish I had all the answers. All I can do is tell you to trust your feelings. And don't worry about what Fang or anyone else thinks. Whatever you do, I support you. I'm here for you, okay?"

I so wanted to believe her. I wanted to believe she no longer wanted to take over the flock, to be the leader instead of me. "Believe me, Max," she whispered.

64

MANY THINGS IN America are really big. Big Macs, for example. And stretch pants, and cars. Not so much in Europe. In general, things there seem to be scaled down, more people sized. And it's charming. It's approachable.

Except when your hotel's only elevator is maybe two feet by two feet and is apparently powered by aging chipmunks running frantically, and you're stuck in it with someone who *stomped on your heart*. Because you chose not to walk up the stairs like a sensible person.

I stood as far away from Fang as possible, which was about four inches, and looked down at my feet. I feigned huge interest in my sneakers and the fact that one of them was held on my foot with bent paper clips because the shoelace had broken.

"So, the whole Doomsday Group thing is getting pretty creepy," Fang said lamely above the sound of the wheezing elevator cables. I wondered when they had last been inspected. This building dated from the late 1600s, a plaque downstairs said. Had the cables been replaced since then?

"Max?" Fang asked.

My head snapped up. I couldn't avoid this anymore. I took a deep breath and let it out slowly. "You figure?" I said. "What with the whole *everyone must die* shtick?"

Fang sighed, and I tried unsuccessfully to inch away from him.

"The flock looks to be in good shape," he said after a moment. "I know you're worried about your mom and Ella." Someone must have filled him in on everything that had been quietly plaguing me for days. I'd been keeping all of that to myself.

I nodded. This superficial conversation was torture. This was the person I'd spent countless hours with, kissing, talking to about everything in our hearts, our minds. How was it that it suddenly felt like Dylan was the one whom I'd known forever and Fang was the total stranger? I knew that life as a genetic experiment sucked, but I hadn't realized just how much worse it might suck as a teenage genetic experiment.

"So...you're not going to talk to me anymore?" Fang sounded angry.

And then, something inside me snapped. "How could you stop loving me?"

As soon as my words came out, they hung in the air between us, and I wanted to disappear. The sound of hurt in my voice, even asking him that question—it was like painting a big target on my chest. I looked away and shrugged, like, *never mind,* but of course it was too late. Once spoken, words can't be unspoken.

Fang smacked his hand against the elevator wall, no doubt startling the chipmunks.

"Is that what you think?" he asked. "Do you think I like seeing you with that…experiment?"

Okay, pot calling the kettle black, but—

"Do you think I like seeing you with that…*clone?*"

"But this is what you decided!" he said.

"This is what *you* decided!" I said, stung. "You're the one who left! You're the one who immediately replaced all of us! Replaced me!"

"She's not a replacement for you!" His face softened for a moment. "No one could replace you. But I needed another good fighter. And…she's really very different from you, in lots of ways."

"That's special!" I snapped. "Glad to hear it!"

"What about you and superboy?" Fang demanded. "You think I don't know what's going on?"

"Yeah? Then tell me, 'cause I have no freaking idea what's going on!"

Our voices had gotten louder and louder in the tiny space, and the elevator had been moving so slowly that we didn't even notice when it groaned to a halt. But suddenly the doors opened, and our voices spilled out into the elegant hallway. Then my eyes locked on Angel's small, determined face.

She crossed her arms and had obviously been waiting for us. "Okay, you guys," she said briskly, "you can argue later. Right now you need to listen up. I have a plan."

Oh, there you go, I thought in dismay. If there were ever words guaranteed to strike fear into my heart...

I sighed.

"Let's hear it," I said.

65

I ALMOST DIDN'T want to let Fang join us in our hotel room. Part of me was tempted to say, "I think your gang is waiting for you on the next floor." But if we were going to battle the Doomsday Group, we all had to work together. So I gritted my teeth while he went to get the others, and then we all crammed into the room that Nudge, Angel, and I shared.

"But—she's seven," I heard Star whisper. "Why does she have a plan?"

I didn't bother to explain.

"Okay, we've seen that the Doomsday Group is made up of young people," Angel said, pacing back and forth. "Like, *really* young people. But . . . I'm the right age to actually join them."

"Join them?" Nudge asked. "How?"

"Let myself be recruited," Angel said, leaning against one of the beds. "They're way less likely to suspect anything from an innocent-looking little girl. Teenagers aren't innocent-looking, ever. And as an actual member, I could get much deeper. I could really get inside and find out much more, I bet."

"But…" Holden looked around. "Maybe an older kid should do it. It's probably pretty dangerous." I didn't mention the fact that he looked about ten himself.

"I can deal with pretty dangerous," Angel said, not bragging, and Fang's gang looked surprised.

I sat there, straining to keep my mouth shut, which just goes to show that a person can change. I was having my typical knee-jerk reaction, which meant I wanted like crazy to keep everyone I cared about safe, nixing ideas and squashing risky plans to make that happen. Clearly, this was a risky plan. I wanted to squash it. I wanted to squash it really, really bad.

But I wasn't going to.

The old me, dealing with the old Angel, definitely would have. And for good reason. But… I'd changed. And so had Angel. And the changed part of me felt that I should probably, against my better judgment, let Angel do what she wanted. And I believed that the changed part of Angel might not sell me down the river while she did it. Lately, she'd been like her old self, the trustworthy old self. The nonbackstabbing old self. And maybe she needed to prove that to me right now. And maybe I needed her to prove that to me.

Slowly I nodded, forcing words out of my mouth. "I think...that's a good idea," I said, shocking everyone. "You're the perfect mark for their indoctrination, and an insider could get a lot of useful information. Yes, it could be a real danger fest, but, as you said, you can handle that."

Angel looked at me with shining eyes, and I got a nice warm feeling inside.

"Wait a second," Ratchet said. "She's a pip-squeak! Those are seriously crazy people! There's no way this should happen!"

"I agree," said Kate.

"I'm pretty tough," Angel said mildly.

"But, still," Kate protested.

"I think it's a good idea," said Maya, though no one had asked her opinion. At all. She nodded at Angel. "You can pull it off."

Angel looked at Fang. She didn't need his approval. But it would be nice to have—they both knew that.

"Yeah," said Fang, running a hand through his shorter-than-I'm-used-to black hair. "Good idea. Just be careful, 'kay?"

"'Kay." Angel beamed, first at him, then at me.

"Um," said Holden, "I just don't think—"

"Look, Holden," I said. "You have special powers. So do I. So does everyone in this room. This kid"—I pointed at

ANGEL

Angel—"flies, can breathe underwater, can read minds, can control people, and can fight like Chuck Norris. She'll be okay."

Holden shut up and sat down.

And oddly, while I was reassuring him, I'd reassured myself. I grinned at Angel, and she grinned back.

Now, if only she wouldn't completely betray all of us, we'd be golden.

66

"HOW OLD ARE you?" a teenage boy with short dark hair asked, looking her up and down, not smiling.

"Seven," Angel said. She shifted from foot to foot, her eyes bright and a hopeful expression on her face.

"She was out in the park, by the fountain," said the girl standing next to him.

"What's your name? Where are your parents?" The boy looked suspicious.

"Angelika," said Angel. "My parents are back in America. I'm here with my school." Without changing her facial expression, Angel edged her consciousness next to theirs, sidling up to their minds, quietly listening in.

It took all of her self-control not to jump as a barrage of

static blasted her mind. Jangly, hard-edged thoughts were chopped up by pictures, like bits of a film. Fire raining from the sky. Blood pooling in the street. Terror. But mostly, she received an overpowering sense of fear, a desperate need to belong, false feelings covering up real ones. With great effort, Angel tore her mind away, trying to regulate her breathing. She felt her heart beating hard.

They were in a poorer, much less pretty part of Paris, in an ancient, sunless alley. The kids were blocking her exit, and Angel noticed with alarm construction overhead. She was feeling a little...trapped.

"And you want to save the world, don't you, Angelika?" the girl asked in a soothing voice, her eyes burning into Angel's. They were nearly colorless like Iggy's but... hypnotic. Angel nodded and glanced away, but the girl grabbed her chin and made Angel look at her. Angel had already visited the minds of the cult members once before, at Ella's school. She hadn't expected to feel so weak now. The cult was getting stronger.

"There you are!"

Angel turned to see Gazzy walking up, enjoying an ice-cream cone. She quickly sent him two thoughts: *Angelika. We're here with our school.*

He blinked once, then licked his cone. "Hey, I was looking for you."

What are you doing here? Angel thought at him. *This was my thing. I can take care of myself.*

Gazzy shrugged. "I was worried about you, Angelika."

"Who's this?" The older boy's voice was cold. Angel caught another glimpse of his violent, fiery thoughts.

"My brother, Andrew," Angel said. *Don't look into their eyes, Gazzy. Try to block what they say.* She saw fear on Gazzy's face and freaked out a little. She could do this. The flock needed her to do this.

"Does anyone know you're here?" the girl asked, sounding a little too casual.

"Nope," Gazzy said, shaking his head, eyes downcast. "They're doing some museum today."

The boy nodded at the girl, then they grabbed Angel and Gazzy by the arms and hustled them deeper into the dark alley. They walked past overturned trash cans and piles of broken boxes, saw rats scurrying away from them. The girl flipped open a black pad attached to a wall and pressed her thumb on a button. Locks released, ringing out like gunshots in the quiet alley. The sound startled Angel but she tried to remain calm. She couldn't remember ever feeling so skittish.

"Everybody in," said the girl, pulling open a thick door covered with rusty sheet metal. Angel felt the girl's senses quicken, felt a mix of anticipation, anxiety, and fear.

Angel suddenly thought that she might never make it out. It wasn't quite a vision but... She paused, and Gazzy shot her a worried look.

The dark-haired boy shoved Angel forward. "In you go!"

Then they were in a narrow, dank hallway, lit by harsh

overhead fluorescent lights. As soon as Angel stepped inside, several huge Dobermans lunged at her, snarling and barking. Angel quickly sent them soothing thoughts, telling them she was a friend. They quieted at once.

She looked up to see the two teens and now a grown-up staring at her.

"Who are your friends, Toni?" the man asked the girl. Angel felt his suspicion.

"Angelika and her brother, Andrew," said Toni. "They want to join us."

"Toni, not now," the man said crossly. "Everything is all set. We can't take them."

"Don't make us go back," Angel pleaded. "You have to let us stay!"

"And why should we?" the man asked.

"Because we can't live with them anymore. The normal people," Angel said, slowly extending her wings.

67

"YOU'RE ONE of the birdkids," the man said, much friendlier now, but Angel had the sense that he was reading from a script. "We've heard about you. Take them upstairs to Mark," the man told Toni, completely ignoring Gazzy. Angel gave him a sweet smile, and she and Gazzy followed Toni down the hallway.

This building, like so many others in Paris, was centuries old. They shuffled along narrow, winding hallways. The low, ancient doorways were blocked with steel grates. It was certainly well protected. Toni took out a huge key ring and had to open a series of locks at each door. As they went farther into the maze, Angel felt Gazzy's panic rising at the memory of times they'd been locked in cages, and she tried to soothe him.

Toni took Angel and Gazzy past several closed wooden doors, and Angel heard people singing: "The One Light is shining on me. The One Light makes everyone free..."

Finally, they emerged in what seemed to be an abandoned factory. A few bare lightbulbs did little to brighten the ominous darkness of the enormous space.

Several kids of different ages stood near a copy machine, bundling flyers. Some sat on the floor, folding flyers in thirds, then stapling them. They all looked gaunt and kind of unhealthy, though they had sort of a bright look in their eyes. Except for one kid, that is. He was banging his head against the wall, over and over, blood streaming down his face.

"Wha-what's with him?" Gazzy stammered in a small voice.

Toni smiled. "Oh, don't mind Allen. He just needs to learn to trust the One Light."

Angel tried to listen to random thoughts, but she pulled back from the compulsive, panicky minds she tapped into: *Be perfect be perfect be perfect be perfect...* This place was seriously giving her the willies.

Toni stopped in front of a crusty, black door, where an older kid seemed to be standing guard. The kid nodded at Toni, then Toni knocked.

"Come in!" a man's voice boomed.

When Toni opened the door, Angel was hit with a blast of malevolence, greed, and lust for power, all overlaced with an oily charm. Angel swallowed hard and held

Gazzy's hand. It took every ounce of her willpower to force herself into that room. She tried to look wide-eyed and innocent, but her throat hurt, the dry, stale air almost choking her

Toni shoved Angel ahead of her, through tall stacks of yellowing newspapers, until they came to an open, dimly lit area. A man stood there, his hands clasped behind his back. He was studying a wall covered in newspaper clippings, and a world map with cities circled in thick black marker. He had just tossed a crumpled sheet of newspaper into the open door of a nearby furnace that was throwing off heat worthy of Hades.

"Toni!" the man said as he turned, narrowing his eyes. "You know we've reached our quota. Are you going against my wishes?"

Toni shook her head. "No, Mark! Of course not!" she said quickly. "Rob sent me here with these two! I would never go against your wishes!"

The man turned and looked directly at Angel. He seemed very old, even though his face was smooth and wrinkle free. But there was not that smiling emptiness that Angel had seen in other DG-ers. Angel sensed such pure evil that she held her breath and tried not to flinch.

"No, of course not," Mark said, smiling like the Cheshire cat. "You believe in the One Light. You want to be part of the solution, not the problem, don't you, Toni?"

"Yes, Mark," Toni said frantically. Angel could feel Toni's terror and saw incoherent orange light glowing menacingly in her mind. "I believe in the One Light. You know I do."

"Good girl," said Mark, and Angel felt Toni almost weep with relief.

Toni turned to Angel and Gazzy and pushed them forward. "Show him," she said. Summoning her courage, Angel stepped closer, urging Gazzy to stay behind her as she carefully opened her wings.

"Oh, that's good," Mark almost purred. "That's very good. Your wings will bring great strength to many of our children."

Angel wondered just exactly what *that* was supposed to mean. Especially when the next thing Mark did was to pull a hot, glowing poker from the furnace nearby.

"Let's see if we can trust you," he said, moving toward her.

68

THE DOOMSDAY GROUP posters announced that D-day was near, that when the world ended, the new regime would begin.

Why aren't crazy people content to take over, like, one town? It always has to be the whole world. They can't just control maybe twenty people. They have to control everyone. They can't just be stinking rich. They have to be incomprehensibly stinking rich. They can't just do genetic experiments on a couple unlucky few. They have to put something in the water. In the air. To get everyone.

I was tired of all of it.

But if their claims were true, this could be the worst thing we'd ever come up against. I couldn't take the chance. What was really getting to me was that since Angel and

Gazzy had left yesterday afternoon, we hadn't heard from them. All sorts of bad scenarios played out in my brain, but I hoped if they'd been harmed, I would somehow know it, feel it.

"What time does the rally start?" Dylan asked.

"You saw the poster. Noon," I said, my anxiety making me cranky.

His eyes met mine, and his expression told me that he understood, that he didn't take it personally. Just then I remembered being with him atop the Arc de Triomphe. Being held, being comforted again wouldn't be such a bad thing right now.... I looked away, angry at myself for thinking like a weak and weepy damsel.

"We should go there early," said Nudge, fidgeting in her chair. Despite all the baddies and dangers and disasters we'd faced, this one felt different. We were all on edge.

I nodded. "We'll head there right after breakfast—and try to volunteer."

Fang's gang had its own plan; our part was to get jobs at the rally.

By 10:00 a.m., crowds were gathering at the Place de la Concorde. It was a huge plaza and could hold thousands of people. Somehow the DG had gotten permission to close off the traffic circle around the tall pink-marble obelisk that had been a gift from Egypt nearly two hundred years before.

The DG had plastered the place with flyers, promising a wonderful rally, filled with truth, enlightenment, and new beginnings, all starting at noon.

"Truth, enlightenment, and new beginnings? Try mass destruction of humanity!" Dylan sputtered.

I nodded, continuing to scan the area. I saw nothing ominous—and no signs of Angel or Gazzy. How would D-day come about? A bomb? Death rays? A huge meteor that no one expected? So far I wasn't getting any clues. I felt tense, with a weird sense of foreboding in the pit of my stomach. Still, this could all turn out to be a huge bust. Maybe the DG had overextended itself?

I could only hope.

We found the main stage, where kids were setting up metal barriers to control the crowd. At least six news vans were unloading equipment, getting ready to film whatever happened.

"Why haven't we heard from Angel and Gazzy?" I asked under my breath as we waited to speak to someone in charge. "I'm getting nothing from her."

"I'm sure she's okay," Dylan said, putting a hand on my shoulder. I tried not to jump out of my skin. Would I ever get used to him? It really seemed like too much, to have to deal with my feelings about him on top of saving the world.

"Yes?" A smiling teenage girl came to the metal barrier. She looked normal, 100 percent human. Though that didn't mean anything. "Can I help you?"

"We'd like to volunteer," I said eagerly. "This is so exciting!"

"It really is," said the girl. "I feel so honored to be here today serving the One Light." She gave us another smile. "We're lucky to have all the help we need right now, so why don't you grab a good spot and wait for the rally to begin? We're going to have multiple live feeds to just about every major city in the world—and then a huge fireworks display at the end!"

"I love fireworks!" Nudge said cheerfully.

"It's going to be beautiful!" The girl's eyes sparkled. "Mark is going to deliver a really inspiring message."

"I know!" I tried to sound perky. It was hard. "That's why we really want to be part of this. We came all the way from the US of A to help! Isn't there anything we can do?"

"I'm not sure what else there is," the girl said, smiling helplessly. "I'm sorry."

"We were thinking that maybe a cool aerial show would help advertise the rally," I said quickly. "We could show people how special it is to be different—or enhanced."

Dylan stepped back and quickly extended his wings, fifteen feet of bones, muscle, and raw power. The girl almost fell over backward.

"Oh, yes," she said in awe. "I think an aerial show is a brilliant idea!"

69

HALF AN HOUR LATER, we were gliding and swooping over the Place de la Concorde on a gorgeous sunny morning in Paris. If we weren't there trying to stop a bunch of crazies from blowing up the world, it would have been great.

As it was, the closer it got to noon, the more people poured into the enormous plaza, and the more I realized just how many people might lose their lives right in front of me if we couldn't figure out what was going on and how to stop it.

The four of us (me, Dylan, Nudge, and Iggy) pulled out all the stops: we dive-bombed the crowd, making them scream; we did death spirals around the obelisk (that I hoped were not omens); we shadowed flocks of pigeons and imitated their movements. It seemed like everybody in the plaza had their eyes glued on us, spellbound, making anyone engaged in nefarious activity easier for us to spot.

Throughout everything, I maintained a raptor lookout for Angel and Gazzy, lasering in on everyone working around the stage, every member of the DG I saw. Fang and his gang were in plain view—well, not Star so much, what with all the zipping around. They were handing out copies of the Enhanced People's Manifesto, selling T-shirts, and generally walking about, and, we hoped, gathering some intel.

An emcee had taken the stage and was starting to whip the crowd into a frenzy, announcing their special lineup, the musical guests, and the huge fireworks display at the end.

But still no Angel or Gazzy.

Dylan and I were flying in tight formation, moving our wings with split-second precision so we wouldn't crash. I wondered if Fang had noticed or if it bothered him. I still noticed Maya. A lot. Every time I saw her, it was like getting salt water in my eyes all over again.

Suddenly, I realized that Dylan had shifted his position to fly barely two feet above me, matching me wing stroke for wing stroke.

"What are you doing?" I asked, craning to look up at him.

"I like this view," he said.

I frowned. "What do you mean?"

"I like watching your...power," he said. "You're a beautiful flyer. Your hair is streaming through the air like silk ribbon. The sun is shining on your feathers. And I'm just glad to be here, with you. Even if we are trying to stop mass destruction."

My face burned. Once again, when I was feeling at my most vulnerable, Dylan was somehow there, saying exactly the right thing, reading my mind—

"Can you read minds?" I asked.

"No," Dylan said. "Not that I would tell you if I could." He gave me an infuriating smile and then rose higher in the air, looking graceful and strong.

Everything was so messed up.

Max!

I almost looked around but then realized that I was hearing Angel's voice in my head.

Angel? I thought, studying the crowd anxiously. *Where are you? Are you okay? What's going on?*

Danger, Angel told me. *Max, such enormous danger, I can't even tell you. We're in the sewers, beneath the city. We've never faced anything like this. I'm scared, Max.*

My heart pounded in my chest as I scanned the city streets below. *Where are you??* I thought.

Under the Place de la Concorde, Angel told me. Her thoughts were fuzzy, indistinct.

Just then, my eyes focused on a small black dot, right

252

outside the barricades around the plaza. It was an open manhole cover, maybe two feet in diameter.

Angel was there. I was sure of it.

I tucked my wings against my back, angled down, and shot toward the small opening at a hundred miles an hour.

I'm on my way, I thought.

70

TRYING TO FLY through a target that small was like trying to spit from the top of the Empire State Building to hit a nickel on the ground below. But I'd done it before, and I knew I could do it again. I just needed to focus. And for everyone to stay the heck out of my way.

Max, maybe you shouldn't come down here. I don't know if we can fix this, Angel's fuzzy, troubled thought said to me. *There's just too much. This might be... the end.*

I couldn't even think as I plunged downward. I tucked my wings back tight, pointed my hands forward, and dove into the darkness.

As soon as I was through, I tucked myself into a ball and flung my wings out wide. I hit a hard concrete floor and tumbled, scraping my face and hands, but my sneakers and my wings helped me stop. I skittered forward, slightly out of control, and halted just inches from the narrow canal that flowed through the sewer system.

Whew, I thought, then heard a whoosh. Something big and heavy plowed into me from behind and shoved me right into the water.

"Augh!" I said, as it followed me over the edge and landed in the water with a splash.

I could see Dylan well enough to whack him hard on the shoulder.

"Thanks! A girl always loves to take a dip in the sewer!" I said.

He scrambled onto the bank and held out his hand to help me up. I ignored it and got out by myself.

"What are you doing here?"

We spoke at the exact same time, the exact same words. He answered first.

"Saw you go down," he said. "Followed you."

I tried to shake some water off. "I got a message from Angel," I said, scanning the tunnel. "She says there's massive danger down here, something too big for us to fix or deal with."

"So of course you immediately came down."

"Yeah. That's the way it works in the flock," I said. "And you just left Nudge, Iggy, and Total alone up there?"

Dylan shook his head. "Fang and Maya showed up, just as you took your dive. They said they'd stay with them."

Max? Angel's voice trembled inside my head.

I turned this way and that, as if I could get a trajectory on a thought. *Where are you?* I asked her.

There was a long pause, then Angel said, *This way.*

I just slowly tried to follow her thought, and when it felt right, I started walking.

"What kind of danger? Did she say?" Dylan asked quietly.

I shook my head, trying to listen. The water trickled by in the middle canal. I heard the skittering of small feet, heard the clicks of insects. But nothing else.

This way . . .

"I think she's nearby," I said softly, frustrated. "It's not clear. She's not giving me directions."

"Max." Dylan took my arm. "Are you sure that you're hearing Angel?"

I stopped in my tracks.

After a moment's reflection, I nodded. "It sounds like her," I said. "And not many people can send thoughts."

Dylan hesitated, looking around. "It's just . . . If this is a trap, it's a really good one."

Max?

I hadn't felt Angel seem this frightened in . . . forever.

Where are you? I thought. *What's going on?*

I can't ever tell you, Max, Angel responded. *Not ever. Just that now I know for sure what kind of evil they're capable of.*

71

WE'RE COMING, ANGE, I thought. Later I'd find a way to get her to tell me what they did to her.

The concrete was smooth, wet, and slimy, requiring careful foot placement. My heart was pounding, and I felt jittery with dread. At first I thought the dull roar I heard was water rushing somewhere. But as we walked, I realized it was the sound of the crowd above us. The rally was heating up.

Which meant time was running out.

"I hope these tunnels are sturdy," Dylan whispered. "There are probably five thousand people up there. At least."

I nodded. I couldn't tell exactly what was happening, but the waves of sound swelled and receded as the crowd got more and more excited about the Doomsday Group's message.

Again, Dylan took my arm. He leaned down and spoke into my ear, almost inaudibly. "Up ahead. To the left. They're behind that wall."

I glanced into his eyes—he looked certain but cautious.

We flattened out against the wall and sidled forward, moving noiselessly, breathing very slowly, totally in sync with each other. Another five yards. Then I thought I heard Gazzy's voice.

"Just ten," he said.

"No," said Angel.

"Five."

"No."

I shot a knowing look at Dylan but had too much experience to feel glad yet. They could be in cages. This actually could be a trap. Any number of awful things could still happen.

Slowly, I edged around the corner, listening so hard my ears hurt. The screams, chants, and clapping overhead were starting to drown out everything down here. With Dylan behind me, I sank down to my knees and eased forward so I could see.

Gazzy and Angel were alone in a huge, cavernlike room that reminded me of the subway tunnels in New York City. There was a grate of metal bars at the entrance, but it had been left open, as if someone had left in a hurry. I stood up and stepped forward.

Angel saw me first. "Max!" I saw relief on her face, but she remained quite still, and I soon saw why.

She was completely surrounded by explosives.

72

"MAX!" SAID GAZZY. "Look!" He waved his arms at piles and piles of what looked like Silly Putty. Big, huge bricks of Silly Putty. Which had wires running to them. On the wall was a digital clock with large red numbers. It was counting down.

The sewer tunnels beneath the Place de la Concorde, where thousands of people were awaiting their "new beginning," were packed with enough C-4 to make a crater the size of Texas. France is a bit smaller than Texas.

"Thank God you're okay, Ange," I said, my throat tight. "Did they hurt you?"

"I'll tell you later," said Angel. "Time is running out. Gazzy and I came down here to check out some stuff we overheard at the DG headquarters and—"

"Max," Gazzy broke in, practically vibrating with excitement. "Have you ever seen so many explosives?"

"No," I said. "Not even close."

"I guess this is the big fireworks display they were talking about," Dylan said.

Suddenly a new voice spoke out of the darkness. "I bet you're right."

The four of us spun around. We assumed battle positions even as my brain realized that it was Fang, that he must have followed us, and that fighting in a room full of plastic explosives was probably not a good idea.

"Where did you come from?" I asked, rattled.

"I saw you go down," said Fang. "I came to help." My sense of pride flared up, then quickly faded. The days when I preferred to fight the bad guys with one wing tied behind my back were gone. The more help, the better.

"Could I maybe...just keep ten chunks?" Gazzy asked wistfully. "Small ones?"

"No," Dylan, Fang, and I all said in unison.

"Okay, I'm seeing a lot of plastique, and it's wired to a detonator," I said. C-4 by itself is actually pretty stable. It needs something to ignite it before it will explode. "But what's in these big metal tanks?"

"It's marked VX — *gaz toxique*," Angel said.

"Is that a cute French way of saying we're surrounded by a completely lethal gaseous nerve agent?" I asked.

Angel nodded unhappily.

Perfect. A quick glance around showed almost as much

poison gas as explosives. "When the C-4 detonates, the VX will be released too," Dylan realized.

"All those people above us," I said, the full horror slowly sinking in.

"These sewer pipes go all over," said Gazzy. "Some of them go out into the ocean, and some go into Belgium and Germany. They're really old, and they all seem connected. They'll carry the poison pretty far away, and it'll seep up through drainage grates."

"Is there any way to dismantle the timers?" Fang asked.

"They're complicated," Gazzy said, "but I've seen them before. I wish Iggy were here."

"We can grab him," I said, but Fang shook his head.

"When I left him, he and Nudge were circling back with Maya to find the gang. We'll never reach them in time."

"What does that timer say?" I asked.

Gazzy looked. "Seven minutes."

"Is that enough time for you to kill it?" Fang asked.

"I think so," Gazzy said. He traced a set of colored wires from one timer to the next. "I can probably do it in about five minutes. I've always wanted to work on one of these."

I was torn and looked at Fang. He understood: Gazzy could stay and try to save everyone, possibly sacrificing himself in the process...or I could order him out of here, saving my whole flock but sentencing thousands of innocent people to certain death.

It was my call. Because I was the leader.

I'm great at thinking on my feet and making snap decisions, but this—this was a big life-or-death choice. I felt stuck. And every second counted.

Dylan touched my back gently, as if to tell me that he knew it was hard, but he'd understand whichever way I went. At least, I hope that's what he meant.

"I think Gazzy should stay," Angel said, looking up at me. "And I'll stay with him, to help. I'm not as good as Iggy, but I can do whatever he tells me to."

"No, not you too," I said.

"I'll stay," said Fang. "With three of us, we'll make it work." He turned to Gazzy. "Get going. Be fast but careful."

"Fang is right," said Dylan.

I realized I couldn't fix this situation. I couldn't make the perfect decision that would save everyone. I had to trust their instincts. And I had to do what I could.

"We need to go warn everyone in the plaza," I said, trying to kick my brain into gear. "We need to get as many people out of there as possible."

I didn't say it, but we were all thinking the words *just in case.*

Angel nodded. "Yes. You guys get going!" She looked at me one last time. "It'll be okay, Max. I'll be with you always, no matter what. And Max—I believe in you. *Forever.*"

73

DYLAN AND I raced down the tunnel as fast as we could. I was overjoyed to see the shaft of light coming from the open manhole.

"How do we fly up through that?" Dylan asked as we skidded to a halt.

I grabbed a ladder rung set into the cement wall. "We climb!"

Once we were out, the normalcy of the street scene made what we'd encountered below seem even more surreal. Without worrying who might see us, we launched ourselves into the air and rocketed back to the stage in the middle of the Place de la Concorde.

Iggy and Nudge—no Maya in sight—were still flying,

performing for the audience. Onstage, I saw an older teen-age girl, talking into a headset, walking around, smiling.

"You want to be saved, don't you?" she said.

"Yes!" the crowd roared.

"You want to be safe in the arms of the Earth Mother when the apocalypse comes, don't you?"

"Yes!!"

"And you, your children, and your children's children will be safe, will be saved forever, because of the choices you make today," said the girl, turning serious. Then she smiled and walked to the other side. "And what's the way to the future?"

"The One Light!" the crowd roared. They were practically hysterical with excitement, and I wondered if they'd been given some type of drug. I couldn't tell. All I saw were beaming faces, fists raised in the air, people waving signs, "Kill the Humans" T-shirts.

T minus five and a half minutes. Let's get this show on the road.

I aimed down at the stage, and the girl caught sight of me. "Look, everyone!" she shouted into the microphone. "That's the future of the human race! Enhanced is where it's at! That's the promise of the One Light!"

The crowd cheered and applauded for my enhanced self.

I continued flying at full speed, and the girl's expression went from delight to confusion to concern in a matter of seconds as I streaked toward her. I buzzed her close enough to mess up her hair, then grabbed the cordless mic out of her hand.

"Everyone! There are bombs under this plaza!" I shouted with no preamble. "You have minutes, maybe seconds to save yourselves! Everyone get out of here as fast as possible! There are bombs and poison gas under the plaza!"

I glanced at the girl. Where I'd expected to see outrage, anger, excuses thrown out at the audience to keep them there, there was...nothing. Just smiling, serene, calm. She'd known about the impending disaster awaiting the crowd, awaiting her, and she'd just accepted it.

Her tranquil smile tore at my heart like long, icy fingers. It was terrifying.

Scanning the faces of the crowd was even worse. I'd banked on screaming people swarming the exits like frightened cattle, knocking down the metal barricades. Or at the very least, some vague murmurs of alarm. Instead, they were nodding at me like puppets on strings, smiles painted into place.

The icy feeling within me was growing. They wanted to die. Every last one of them.

"This is a trap!" I bellowed at them, frantic. "There are bombs under this plaza! *Bombs* and *poison gas!* Don't you get it? Get out of here! Scram! Save yourselves!"

"Save the planet! Kill the humans!" they chanted. "Support the future of enhanced society!"

Dylan swooped beside me and grabbed the microphone. "How are you going to get enhanced if you're all blown up into little pieces?" he yelled.

They actually cheered.

Every ounce of energy seemed to leak out of me, and I felt like giving up right then. If everyone wanted to go up in one big firework, who was I to snuff out the spark? But then I glanced over and saw the determined look on Dylan's face as Nudge and Iggy dropped onstage for backup, and I remembered who I was and what I was here for.

These freaks might have thought they were saving the world, but that was my job, and they were going to play by my rules. Which didn't involve any of that "Kill the Humans" crap.

Fight time!

74

THEN A SORT of riot broke out, but it wasn't the out-raged, we-don't-want-to-die kind we'd hoped for. A bunch of the One Lighters jumped onstage and made a beeline for us, mumbling about "merging with the promise of enhancement."

Truly horrific.

Nudge and Iggy were going all Fight Club on some of the DG guards, who were heavily muscled, as if they'd already received enhancements. But it wasn't those dudes that were giving them trouble. My flock were pros. A roundhouse kick here, a karate chop there, and the guards were toast. It really was just like riding a bicycle.

No, it was the kids—the culties—who were the real problem. Picture Michael Jackson in that "Thriller" video, surrounded by flesh-craving zombies closing in. That was us, but our dead-eyed suicidal zombies all had angelic grins pasted on their faces as they pawed at our wings. It was like they wanted to *claim* us. Ick.

The mob was a living, breathing sponge, hundreds of kids deep. And after spending my developmental years in a cage…Claustrophobia? I *has* it. They were clutching at us, pulling on our feathers, touching our arms and our faces. How do you fight a swarm of sickos who want to die and don't mind taking you with them?

And all this while the countdown to D-day continued.

I was panicking, really panicking, for the first time in…at least a few days. And as I glanced around, the over-whelmed faces of Dylan, Iggy, and Nudge were not the least bit reassuring.

Right on cue, Maya showed up, gang in tow. They were able to rip through the crowd, in part because at first the culties didn't seem to understand that the gang was enhanced as well.

Kate grabbed armfuls of Doomsday kids, four or five at a time, and hurled them out the exits. When she'd cleared a pathway through the crowd for us, she picked up two huge, lumbering guards and swung them upside down by their feet, one in each hand, while Nudge boxed their noses, dodging the rush of blood. With space cleared, we could use our wings again and attack from above.

Meanwhile, Ratchet seemed to sense every attacker coming his way, and, on top of that, seemed to be kicking it at some old-fashioned hand-to-hand combat. He had teamed up with Iggy, who was a natural spinning, whirling dealer of pain as he punched, kicked, and chopped his way through an onslaught of guards. They both looked pretty happy.

And Star, the blond girl, had hit on the biggest jackpot of all, sort of by accident. She was using her hummingbird speed to flit in circles around the guards, who looked so dizzy and confused that it was almost kind of pathetic.

But the key thing was that when she was zipping around, she was making this high-pitched noise—a supersped-up "Aiiyah!"—that seemed to crack the Doomsday code of brainwashing. The kids were covering their ears, but that sound, and some common sense, was getting through. Star had done for these kids in ten seconds what it had taken Angel hours of mind-coaxing to accomplish: They were... snapping out of it. And running for the exits.

Huh. Wish we'd figured that out sooner!

With the mob no longer singing Killmas carols, maybe we could wrap up this little party and make sure Gazzy and Angel were safe. Though with Fang there, of course they were. He wouldn't have left them—

Right then, Ratchet signaled to us, and Dylan spied something I couldn't quite see off to the side of the stage. His face twisted with rage as he pushed me out of the way.

"Look—" he started to say, then suddenly his voice cut out, and I saw him spin like a top. Blood started flowing to the ground, spurting like drops of rain.

75

"DYLAN!" I SCREAMED. I knelt down beside him, feeling pukey and fuzzy and like the wind had been knocked out of me. He was holding his arm (sigh of relief) tight, grimacing. Blood leaked out through his fingers.

"It's fine," Dylan said tersely. "Bullet went right through—bone seems okay."

I didn't even have a second to give him my best *I'm-really-glad-you-didn't-just-die-because-I-kind-of-like-you-more-than-I-thought* look though, because—

"*Max, watch out!*" Dylan shouted and shoved me. Stage right, an older man with wild hair and plastic-like skin was firing a gun at us.

"Mark, no!" shouted Beth, the Queen of the Cult. Big of her.

The guy pushed the girl aside and aimed, and I dodged a bullet that came close enough to nick my feathers. I tried to drag Dylan out of the way, but the guy was still popping off as many shots as he could.

"Max, go! Don't protect me!" Dylan yelled. "Go!"

Then, Holden, the little Fang gang kid, came out of nowhere with an apparent death wish. He raced directly toward the maniac with the gun shrieking something that sounded like "*I am Starfishhh!*"

Holden looked like Swiss cheese for a second as Mark used up the last of his ammo, but the holes on the kid's arms closed up in seconds flat. This little daredevil had some serious chops, and by now most of the flock and the gang were closing in. The gunman, looking more than a little freaked out, ran offstage like a five-year-old girl.

I was still leaning over Dylan—the bullet hole was already healing, and he had some color back in his face—when someone cut in.

"Need a hand?" Fang asked. Dylan looked at the hand wearily, but took it, pulling himself up.

I raised an eyebrow at Fang.

He shrugged. "What? I'm trying to learn to be a team player." Dylan actually smiled and, get this, fist-bumped my ex.

I nodded, a little dazed, and moved to the other side of the stage to herd out more of the confused former One Lighters.

It was actually kind of amazing to see two of the guys I

cared most about in the world, different in so many ways, fighting together side by side. Fang covered Dylan's weak side, and together they were doing some serious damage. *We've come a long way, baby,* I was musing, when suddenly a heavy weight hit me in the back.

Then two viselike hands clamped around my neck.

76

"YOU COULD HAVE ruled your own country!" Mark, the cowardly shooter, yelled into my ear. Lesson number one: megalomaniacs never give up when they should.

I tried to rise up on my hands and knees, but the guy was on my back and weighed a ton.

"Whoa!" I coughed, struggling to breathe. "What'd you get enhanced with—ham?"

"You could have been a princess in the New World! But now you're going to die like a lowly, ordinary human." He practically spat the last word, though he appeared to be human himself—a heavily Botoxed, steroid cocktail of a human, but a human nonetheless. This guy needed an intense course on overcoming self-hatred, stat.

"The thing about being a princess," I managed to say,

still struggling to get out from underneath him, "is that ... you have to ... kiss ... a lot of ... *frogs!*"

He was strong, and I clawed at his fingers with shockingly little effect. He clamped down harder on my windpipe, and I started to get really worried. I heard blood rushing in my ears, heard my heartbeat slowing. Not good.

This wasn't how it was supposed to end.

"You are a black cloud over the One Light," I heard the man say, as if from a distance. "You won't destroy everything I've worked for and planned for all these years!"

Suddenly my head got yanked to one side, and the vise grip around my neck slackened a bit. I pried off his fingers with difficulty as I heard his voice, full of hatred and rage, shrieking, then a rush of air whooshed into my lungs so fast it was almost painful. I gasped like a fish, sucking in air with a wheeze, and then I heard my voice snarl, "That's not how it's going to end, dirtbag!"

I got up on all fours, wobbly, my head starting to clear.

But it hadn't been my voice after all. It had been Maya's. She had broken off a piece of a metal barricade and beaned ol' Mark with it as hard as she could.

Of course, Mark, pumped up with who knows what, survived the blow. With an angry bellow, he got to his feet as I stumbled out of the way. Maya hauled back and smashed the metal pole into Mark again. There was an awful *thwock*.

"You know," I choked out, "the bigger they are ..." I

lined myself up with Maya and grabbed the other end of the pole.

"The harder they fall!" Maya said, and the two of us rushed Mark using our combined strength to clobber him one more time. He staggered backward, looking surprised, and just as he started to look angry, he fell back off the stage, flailing through the air.

He landed ten feet below with a sickening crunch—I'm guessing his enhancements didn't allow him to bounce back up like a ball. We call that a design flaw.

Maya and I looked at each other as I began to wrap my mind around the depressing realization that she had probably just saved my life.

"Max!" Dylan rushed over, and I blinked and looked around. The guards were all taken care of, what was left of my flock was still standing, and the rally had mostly dispersed.

It looked like another job well done. Now I just had to find Angel and Gazzy.

But as I took one last look at Mark's body on the ground, I saw—were those?—wires sticking out below him. He wasn't a bot, we knew that much, so were they connected to—

And that was when the City of Lights exploded with a thunderous *boom!*

77

THE NEXT FEW moments, surprisingly, proved that a lot of what Dr. Hans and the DGs had said was true: those of us with wings and wild-animal DNA were up above the blast in less than two seconds, leaving danger, rubble, and chaos behind. People left on the ground weren't so lucky: those nearby were hurled into the air by the blast, and more were injured by flying debris. Trembling aftershocks also took a toll.

Through the dust and debris, I saw Fang's gang, most of it, outside the plaza. I guessed that Ratchet had sensed what was about to happen, and they were strong enough and fast enough to get to safety quickly.

"Everyone okay?" I barked, and they nodded. Next to

me, Maya did a quick head count. No Fang. Or Gazzy. Or Angel. My adrenaline surged.

"What happened?" I said, scanning the ground anxiously. "Gazzy's *never* not been able to dismantle something!"

"I'm not sensing poison gas," Dylan said, "not that that means anything. It might be odorless and tasteless."

I circled quickly, going lower as the smoke settled. Where the open manhole had been, there was now a huge crater, maybe thirty feet across and thirty feet deep. My heart seized. Where was Gazzy? Angel? Fang?

Suddenly, I saw a smallish birdkid soaring upward, just as another gigantic explosion rocked the street. Shockwaves knocked me back several feet, and I inhaled a bunch of dust.

"Max!" Gazzy's face was black, his eyes wide and scared.

"Gaz! Thank God you're okay! Where's Angel? And Fang?"

Gazzy started choking, forgetting to keep himself aloft, and I drifted down beside him as he landed on the broken granite pavers and rubble. He opened his mouth to speak, but coughed, then tears started running down his cheeks.

"Gazzy! What happened?" I said, but he shook his head, coughing,

Aftershocks rumbled below us again, and I made Gaz take to the air in case of another explosion. He could fly okay, but he looked miserable, and he kept gagging and spitting out dust.

Where was Angel? Where was Fang? I shot a panicked look at Dylan, and he understood immediately, diving down the hole to find them.

Could Angel and Fang really be gone? My brain whirled at the horrible possibility. Gazzy was still wheezing, unable to talk. There were times when I'd thought I'd lost Angel or Fang before. And when Fang left, I never thought I'd ever see him again. But that had felt more like...I wouldn't see him, but he still existed. What about now? How would it feel if he—

I was swallowing shakily, terrified thoughts piercing my brain like shards of glass. Just as Dylan landed on the street, Fang shot up toward me, coming through the billowing clouds of dust and debris. His shirt was shredded, his face bruised and cut. Like Gazzy, he was covered with soot.

"Gaz! You made it out," he gasped, when he got closer.

"Angel was right behind me," Gazzy said. "Right behind me!" He looked around us, everywhere, as if expecting to see his sister making her way toward us.

I flew right up to Fang and clutched him, if only to convince myself that he was really alive.

That intense joy and relief ended in a nanosecond. I pulled back and grabbed his shoulders. "Where's Angel?!"

"I—don't—"

"How could you leave her?" I shrieked.

"Max, I—Gaz was almost done and I thought—Angel said—"

I looked into Fang's face. His dark eyes, usually bottomless, were full of emotion. His face was ashen. My eyes widened and my hands dropped from his shoulders. I let my wings take me backward, away from him, as a silent, searing scream started to rise in my chest. He didn't say anything out loud, but he told me just the same: he didn't know where Angel was, and he was afraid that something awful had happened to her.

My breath caught in my throat, and my blood turned to ice. Had she been trapped by the second explosion? It didn't seem possible. I remembered her small, earnest face, saying, "I can deal with pretty dangerous."

"Angel, where are you?" Gazzy yelled, turning in circles, bobbing up and down in the sky, then suddenly he crumbled, his face dissolving into tears. My munitions and weapons expert really was just a nine-year-old kid, and he'd just lost his little sister.

And I'd lost my baby.

78

"IT'S BEEN FIVE HOURS, Max." Dylan's quiet voice was like sandpaper.

"I refuse to believe that she didn't escape," I said stubbornly, and tried to help superstrong Kate shift some more twisted wreckage from the blast site.

Dylan and I had even crawled through the rubble near the manhole and tried to get back into the sewer system. But the tunnel had completely collapsed, and Gazzy said that while he'd managed to defuse most of the network of bombs, he obviously hadn't gotten to every one, plus the poison gas was still down there.

He'd given me that information through sobs, as I held him, his head on my shoulder.

Angel's last words to me kept replaying in my mind:

It'll be okay, Max. I'll be with you always, no matter what. And Max—I believe in you. Forever. What had she meant by that? Had she had some premonition that she might not come back? Had she made the ultimate sacrifice? She'd talked of all my sacrifices. I was haunted by the idea that she might have chosen to make one of her own.

Next to me, Kate sat down. Star held out a bottle of tepid water, and Kate drank it. She looked exhausted. I sighed and bent down to move another chunk of cobblestone.

The police had closed down the entire area, evacuating the buildings that were still standing, clearing the Place de la Concorde. We'd hovered above the Louvre, waiting for them to leave, after Fang had made sure that his gang was okay. They'd been great, helping to rescue at least twenty people trapped under the rubble, helping to get hurt children to nearby hospitals. Now they sat on a curb, looking wiped, like Nudge, Gazzy, and Iggy. Only Fang, Dylan, and I were still on our feet. Just barely.

An aerial search had turned up nothing, but after two hours we'd found one of Angel's pink sneakers, two blocks away. It had been ripped apart, its sole dangling. A section of it was stained with blood.

That's when I had finally broken down.

"I tried to get to all of them," Gazzy sobbed. "I thought I had. There must have been like a remote setoff that I didn't know about. I don't know what happened." I remembered the wires sticking out of Mark and shuddered.

Would Gazzy ever forgive himself? I was the one who

had decided to let him try. If I had insisted he leave there, made all of the flock get out of there and let the DGers...

We'd all be safe, but thousands of people might be dead, Paris would be even more ruined than it was now, and I'd still never be able to forgive myself.

This was the hard stuff, the leader stuff, the save-the-world stuff that I just couldn't stand having to deal with. At a certain level, there are no best choices, no right decisions. Only choices that are less bad, decisions that are less wrong.

It was dark now. It was hard to accept that we'd found all we were going to find. We'd all been crying, off and on, for hours, except for Fang and Dylan. Somehow they had remained strong as they worked side by side with me, shifting the biggest boulders and the heaviest pipes.

Now I stood looking at the crater, wondering how the DGers could have done such a thing. How could that guy Mark have lived with himself? It was all too much. I wanted to go home, but I wasn't even sure where home was at that point. I didn't even know what had become of my mom or Jeb. Or Ella. Had they been part of this in some way? I wasn't certain about anything anymore.

I hung my head, and I felt someone, Fang, gather me gently to him. My cheek rested on his shoulder, and my silent tears soaked his torn shirt. He felt warm and strong and heartbreakingly familiar. And at that moment, not a single thing in my life was certain, strong, or whole. Nothing.

Least of all Fang.

79

THE WEIRD, WEIRD thing about devastating loss is that life actually goes on. When you're faced with a tragedy, a loss so huge that you have no idea how you can live through it, somehow, the world keeps turning, the seconds keep ticking.

Within hours of Angel's disappearance, while my heart was still raw and bleeding and in denial, Paris was already starting to recover. Cleanup teams swarmed the Place de la Concorde; officials tested radiation levels. Fang had given them information about what still lurked in the crushed tunnels beneath the city, and they'd deployed military experts and bomb squads to finish the job that Gazzy had done so amazingly well, for a nine-year-old.

We'd combed all the hospitals and trauma units,

pushing aside curtains, bursting into rooms, praying we'd see Angel's filthy, wounded face—alive. But we didn't.

As a beautiful sunset painted the area with blood-red hues, people began to pull themselves together. I wanted to grab strangers and yell, "Don't you understand what's happened?" But I knew it was pointless. It was only my pain searching for an outlet.

Finally, Fang came and found me, where I had collapsed in exhaustion, near the blast site. I looked up through dry and mournful eyes. "If we haven't found her body yet, then she's still alive," I said.

He sat down, took my hand in his. Slowly, he shook his head. He looked like he'd aged about ten years in the past twenty-four hours. His face was drawn and gaunt. His hair and clothes were still caked with grit and blood. He shook his head again, slowly.

"No, Max," he said. "Probably not."

I wanted to scream, "It's your fault! You're the one who left her!" But it wasn't his fault. Because I had left all three of them.

"We're...taking off," Fang said.

I knew my face was splotchy and tear stained; my clothes were filthy and covered with soot and blood and dust; my hair was matted with ash and grit.

"What?" I asked dully.

Nudge had been sleeping against my shoulder, and now she roused and blinked groggily.

Fang gestured toward his gang waiting several feet

away. They looked whipped and dirty, and they had new, sad, firsthand knowledge about some of the awful things that can happen in the world. Strangely, seeing them warmed my heart a little. They were starting to look like they belonged with us.

"We're going to take off," Fang repeated. "The cops got some of the DG organizers, but not whoever or whatever was supposed to be the One Light. Gazzy filled me in on what he and—on what he'd learned at their headquarters. So we're going after that. It doesn't sound like Mark was the kingpin—he was only a servant of the One Light."

"Huh," I said, unable to offer more of a reaction.

"We have to kill the plant at the roots," Fang said, "or it'll just grow back."

His face was lined and grim, his voice flat. He'd always loved Angel so much. Like we all had.

"Oh," I said, and I got wearily to my feet, feeling old and hollow and like I would never be happy again. I don't even know what I was expecting, but Fang and I sort of came together in a brief, awkward hug. I clung to him, relishing the milliseconds in his arms like they were hours, then I stepped back.

"So I guess this is it," I said almost incoherently.

"Yeah," Fang agreed, and my heart sank. I'd actually hoped he'd just say *for now*. "Be safe," he said. Then he looked meaningfully at Dylan, as if to say, *"That's your job now—take care of her."*

Maya waited with the gang, and I knew I owed her. I

went and stood in front of her, watching as her eyes met mine.

"Thanks," I told her.

She nodded. And that was it—we were too alike to need anything more.

"Take care, guys," said Fang to the rest of the flock. "I'll post anything I find out on my blog."

More tearful good-byes, and then they were gone. I blinked uncomfortably, feeling grit in my eyes, then turned to the flock. I swallowed hard. "I need to find Ella," I told them. "And my mom. And maybe even Jeb."

Slowly, one by one, they nodded. I let out a deep breath, wondering if I could even get myself airborne.

Dylan came up to me. He wrapped his arm around my shoulder and took one of my hands in his. His hand was large, warm, and comforting. I looked down at it, and again, hot tears pricked the backs of my eyes, then ran down my face, making tracks through the sweat and the blood. I let them fall.

I looked up at him and nodded, and then we got ready to fly.

EPILOGUE
FAMOUS LAST WORDS

"You're very superior, Angel," said a voice.

Angel heard the voice, heard other muffled sounds, but she couldn't open her eyes. She couldn't move a muscle. She tried to still her panic, tried to calm down enough to figure out where she was, what was happening.

Her head was killing her, and she could tell some of her hair was matted with blood. Her feet were bare and cold. She had electrodes taped to her, all over, and as she realized this, panic washed through her. She heard a machine start beeping as her heart beat faster. Not again. She couldn't go through this again.

"It's okay, Angel," said the voice. Angel couldn't tell if a man or a woman was speaking. It sounded like it was coming at her through many layers of cotton. "You're among friends. Even admirers. We're going to take care of you."

Angel tried to speak but couldn't make a single sound. Was she even breathing? She thought so. She realized that her wrist stung—she must have an IV there. It was all nauseatingly familiar: the feeling of helplessness, the smell of disinfectant, the hushed hums and chirps of medical machines tracking every bodily function.

With all of her heart, she wished that she was home with Max and the others, wished she could curl up with Max and watch TV, wished she could watch Ella and Iggy bake cookies. She was just a little kid...

"You see, Angel," the voice continued, "it's important that you recognize your superiority. It's part of your destiny. You have to take strength from that knowledge."

An icy liquid seeped into her hair, and Angel wondered if they were cleaning the blood off.

"When you truly understand your superiority, you'll be able to leave your humanity behind, once and for all. Humans aren't needed for the New World. But superhumans are. Beings that are more than human, better than human. You'll see."

Angel tried sending her thoughts out, tried to get into the heads of whomever was around her. But it was like she was encased in plastic, with no thoughts entering or leaving. She'd never felt more alone. Where was Max? Was she worried? The flock must be going crazy, trying to find her...

She swallowed uncomfortably, aware that a tube was going down her throat.

That was when everything crashed in on her: The bombs, running after Gazzy in the tunnel, the huge explosion. She remembered nothing after that, until just now. She didn't know if Gazzy and Fang had made it out alive. She didn't know if they had saved thousands of people. She didn't even know if she still had a flock.

She thought about the people, so many people, that might be dead right now, because she and Gazzy had failed. *This is my fault,* Angel thought. *All of this is my fault.*

Oh, Max, she thought, sure that Max couldn't hear her. *I'm sorry. I'm sorry.*

Very slowly, a single tear welled up in her closed eye and seeped out from beneath her heavy lid. It rolled down her cheek, past her ear.

"Don't worry, Angel," came the voice again. "You're very special. We're going to take good care of you."

But at least Angel was still human enough to cry.

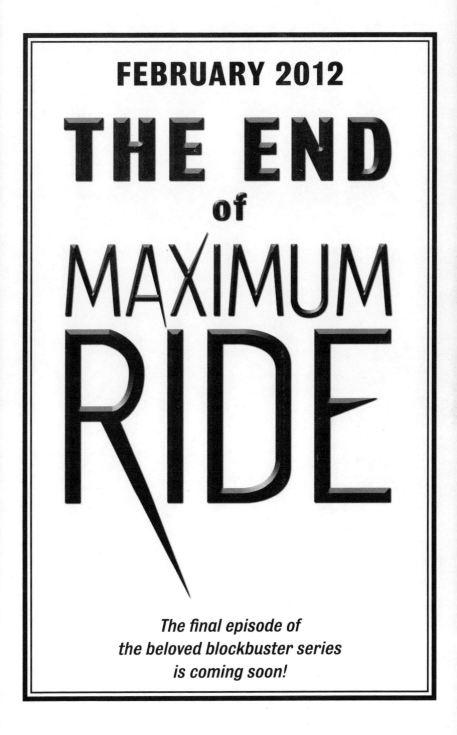

FEBRUARY 2012

THE END

of

MAXIMUM RIDE

*The final episode of
the beloved blockbuster series
is coming soon!*

Whit

HERE'S WHAT HAPPENED, to the best of my shattered ability to recall it.

I do remember that I couldn't have been more lost and alone as I wandered the streets of this gray, crowded, and forsaken city. *Where is my sister? Where are the others from the Resistance?* I kept thinking, or maybe muttering the words like some homeless madman.

The New Order has already disfigured this once beautiful city beyond recognition. It seems like a decaying corpse swelling with mindless maggots. The suffocatingly low sky, the featureless buildings—even the faces of the nervously rushing people flooding around me—are as colorless and lifeless as the concrete under my feet.

I know the general populace has been efficiently brainwashed by the New Order, but these citizens seem a little *too* hushed, a little *too* urgent, a little *too* riveted to the scraps of propaganda clutched in their hands like prayer books.

Suddenly, my eyes spot a word in bold letters on the paper: EXECUTION.

And then the huge video displays hanging above the boulevard light up, and everything becomes clear to me. Every pedestrian stops and stands stock-still, and every head turns upward as if there has suddenly been an eclipse.

On the video screens, a hooded prisoner—small-framed, frail-looking—is kneeling on a starkly lit stage.

"Wisteria Allgood," blares a bone-chilling voice, "do you wish to confess to the use of the dark arts for the wicked purpose of undermining all that is good and proper in our society?"

This can't be happening. My heart is a big lump in my throat. *Wisty?* Did that voice really just say *Wisteria Allgood?* My sister's on an executioner's scaffold?

I grab a slack-jawed adult by his dismally gray overcoat lapels. "Where is this execution happening? Tell me right now!"

"The Courtyard of Justice." He blinks at me irritably, as if I've woken him from a deep sleep. "Where else?"

"Courtyard of Justice? Where's *that?*" I demand of the man, throwing my hands around his neck, nearly losing control of my own strength. I swear, I'm ready to throw this adult against a wall if I have to.

"Under the victory arch—down there," he gasps. He

points at a boulevard that runs off to my left. "Let me go! I'll call the police!"

I shove him and take off running toward a massive ceremonial arch maybe a half mile away.

"You! Wait!" he yells after me. *"Don't I know your face from somewhere?"*

He does. Oh yes. And so would everyone else, if they took the time to notice that there was a wanted criminal running loose in their midst.

But his fellow citizens' eyes remain glued to the screen. They've got an insatiable appetite for malicious gossip of any kind and, of course, an equal taste for senseless death and destruction.

Even when the falsely condemned are kids. Just kids.

I can hear a distant roar now. The sound of hunger— for "justice," for blood.

I forge ahead into the pathetic herd of lemmings. *I'm not going to let them take my sister from me.* Not without a fight to the death anyway.

I round a corner, and then, across the top of the crowd, I see . . . *Is that my sister, Wisty, up on the stage?* She's hooded, dressed all in black, but standing now. Proudly. Brave as ever.

A man—if you would call him that—is on the stage with her. He's leaning on a crooked stick, his wickedly sharp black suit hanging strangely motionless in the wind that's begun to howl through the civic square. His angular face is glowing with smug self-satisfaction, as if he's just devoured a potful of whipping cream.

I know him; I despise him. *The One Who Is The One.* Quite possibly the most evil individual in the history of humanity.

Are there minutes or seconds left before this hideous execution? I have no way of knowing.

I knock people aside as I barrel through the thickening, or should I say *sickening,* throng. I can see a line of well-armed soldiers holding everyone back from the platform. If I can knock one of them down and snatch away a gun...

I look up at the stage just in time to see The One raise his knobby black stick and shake it menacingly at my sister. He has a look of absolute triumph.

"No!" I yell, but I'm unheard in the roaring crowd. They all know what's about to happen. I know, too. I just don't see how I can possibly stop it. There has to be a way.

"Nooo!" I scream. *"You can't do this! This is cold-blooded murder!"*

There's a flash—not of light but somehow of *blackness*—and she's gone. Wisty. My sister. My best friend in the world.

My little sister is dead.

Whit

IF I'M STILL DRAWING air, it's not because I care about living.

The last person in the Allgood family that I knew for certain to be alive, the person who knew me better than anyone else in the world, the person who looked up to me in everything, is *gone*. What an incredible waste of an incredible life.

Wisty died while I watched, and I could do nothing to help her.

The One just vaporized my sister...and that monster, without any hint of conscience, doesn't even seem to have broken a sweat. He throws his arms in the air like he's just scored a goal, like he's mocking the pointlessness of human existence. I go weak in the knees. I feel as if I might throw up as I hear a deafening roar of approval sweep down the concrete canyon of this city—a place that now seems despicable and evil and beyond repair.

The One has just achieved his biggest public relations triumph *ever*. He basks in the adoration—but his usual impatience and anger soon erupt.

"Silence!"

His command sweeps across the city, obliterating every other noise.

But I'm unmoved. Still shell-shocked. Numb everywhere, including in places that I didn't know existed.

"My good citizens," he thunders, without aid of a microphone, "this is a truly magnificent occasion. What you have just witnessed is the obliteration of the last significant threat to our stewardship of the Overworld! Wisteria Allgood, a leader of the Resistance, has just been removed from this dimension. Forever."

He raises his arms again, and a new gust of wind brings a thin layer of ash and the horrible smell of burnt hair across the crowd. These "good citizens" begin cheering again.

I'd collapse to my knees, but I'm surrounded on all sides. Then, suddenly, there is space for me to move. The cheering turns to screaming and the crowd is surging—moving backward—and I see a fiery explosion erupting not fifty yards from where I stand.

I *know* that fire.

"Oh yeah!" I shout as the mere sight of it makes my heart almost burst with joy. *"Oh yeah, oh YEAH!"*

That's my sister! Wisty's alive! She's just set herself on fire, and that, believe it or not, is a good thing.

Wisty

AS SURE AS I am Wisteria Rose Allgood, I have only one thought: *I'm gonna* burn *everything and everyone around me. Burn it all down.*

I'll start with the death-drenched stage, move on to this ridiculously pompous plaza, then hit the whole cold city of stone — this disastrous nightmare of a world. Even if I fry myself to ash in the process, I am going to obliterate all of this, all of them.

The One Who Is The One just killed my friend Margo up on that stage from hell. I recognized her even with a hood over her head. Her purple sneakers and black-and-purple cargo pants were the giveaway. The silver streaks and stars on the sneakers were the final clue. Margo, the last punk rocker on Earth. Margo, the most fearless and dedicated person I've ever known. Margo, my dear friend.

Don't ask me why that monster in the black silk suit was pretending she was me. All I know is that *I'm going to burn that evil madman to cinders.*

So I turn myself into a human torch, just as I have in the past. Only this time I abandon all caution. Suddenly ten-, twenty-, thirty-foot tongues of flame are coursing around me, ripping upward in the formerly cool afternoon air.

The crowd backs away, screaming, and I can't help myself: I smile. I nearly laugh out loud.

And I'm about to turn the heat up another notch—to send jets of fire everywhere around me, to burn brighter and hotter than ever before—when my breath catches in my throat.

I feel *him.* I feel his wretched, diseased mind. I feel his eyes somehow locking on to me.

A thousand soldiers turn my way in unison, and now it's The One who's smiling. He's starting to laugh. And he's laughing at me.

I wince as the air rushes out of me. *How can he have so much power?*

I have no choice but to run, at least to try to escape his wrath.

I throw myself into the panicked human tide, my small frame deftly ducking elbows and shoulders. But The One is too close. I can feel his icy gusts chasing me, reaching out with cold, bony finger–like wisps, grazing my face, my neck, sending a chill so cold it hurts everywhere at once.

I'm starting to think how ironic it is that a firegirl might die in a deep freeze when suddenly I'm smothered by warmth. Somebody grabs me, lifts me up, and nearly squeezes all the breath out of me.

Wisty

IT'S MY BROTHER, Whit.

In a flash, he carries me a hundred, two hundred paces ahead, as if I weigh nothing. Then he and I duck behind a high stone wall. For a few precious seconds, we're out of sight and safe.

I hug Whit with all the strength I have. He finally relaxes his powerful grip enough for me to breathe.

"But if this is really *you*..." He trails off.

"Margo," I whisper. "He killed Margo." Then suddenly I'm crying like a baby. I'm shaking, and my teeth chatter hopelessly.

Margo is *dead*. The girl who helped me put a third piercing in my ear last week. The girl who woke us all up at five a.m. every morning to report for duty, the girl who had more dedication to fighting the oppression of the New Order than the rest of us put together. She was so young. Just fifteen years old.

"I told her not to go in that building without more help. I begged her," my brother says. "Why did she go in there? *Why?*"

"She was always the last to give up on a mission," I remind Whit, as if I'm trying to convince myself that it wasn't our fault she'd been caught. "First in, last out. That was her mantra, right? Stupid!"

"Courageous," he says, and for an instant I see in his eyes why it is that girls love him, why *I* love him. He's honest and sincere and absolutely fearless.

The mission, one of a dozen attempted rescues we'd undertaken in the last month, was our worst failure yet. We were trying to liberate maybe a hundred kidnapped kids from a New Order testing facility. But our intelligence must have been off. Instead of victimized kids, the building held a platoon of New Order soldiers. They were waiting for us.

"Actually, it's lucky *any* of us —," I start to say.

"*Find her!*" The speakers mounted in the plaza start vibrating with The One's irate voice. "There's *another* conspirator in the crowd! She has flaming-red hair! Close the courtyard exits. Capture her *now!*"

Whit grabs a gray hat off a passing businessman and plunks it down on my head.

"Tuck your hair in, quick," he says.

I'm doing just that when a policeman spots me. He's a couple of dozen yards away.

Now he's grabbing for the whistle at the end of a cord

around his neck...and he'll soon have the attention of every soldier in the plaza. Not to mention that of The One, whom I *hate* to mention.

But then a small black figure leaps up and knocks the policeman down flat on his rear.

Whit and I exchange looks of surprise. He says, "Did you just—?"

But before Whit can finish, the black figure—an old woman—is at our side. She presses into my hand a crumpled, gritty piece of paper. "Take it, take it!"

I swear she's the weirdest-looking creature I've ever seen in my life, and yet I *know* her from somewhere.

"Who are—?"

She cuts me off. "Follow this. Go! I'm a friend. Run. Run. Don't stop for a single breath, or it's over. For all of us. *Go!*"

Somehow she gets behind us, and then she delivers a kick to both of our butts. That sends us staggering into the surging crowd.

I immediately turn back...but there's no sign of her.

"You heard her," says Whit. "Go! Now! Go!"

James
Patterson

**To find out more about James Patterson
and his bestselling books, go to
www.jamespatterson.co.uk**

OUT NOW IN PAPERBACK

MAX
A MAXIMUM RIDE NOVEL

James Patterson

NOBODY SAID SAVING THE WORLD WOULD BE EASY.

Until now, Max and the flock have lived a lonely existence: hunted down, tortured, and pushed to the fringe of society. Always on the run, they have never been able to live a normal life. But things are changing.

The flock have finally found acceptance for their extraordinary skills. They don't have to hide away and longer – far from it: now everyone wants to see just what they can do. But fame and fortune always come at a price. Meanwhile, sinister forces are plotting their attack, putting more than just the flock in danger.

Something deadly is lurking in the depths of the ocean. As the flock uncover a terrible secret set to threaten the world, can they save the day or is this a disaster too tough to tackle, even for them?

arrow books

FANG
A MAXIMUM RIDE NOVEL

James Patterson

CAN FANG ESCAPE A TERRIFYING PROPHECY?

Maximum Ride is used to surviving – living constantly under threat from evil forces sabotaging her quest to save the world – but nothing has ever come as close to destroying her as the horrifying prophecy that Fang will be the first to die. Fang is Max's best friend, her soulmate, her partner in leadership of her flock of bird kids. A life without him is a life unimaginable.

Max's desperate desire to protect Fang brings the two closer together than ever. But when a newly created winged boy, the magnificent Dylan, is introduced into the flock, their world is upended yet again. Raised in a lab like the others, Dylan exists for only one reason: he was designed to be Max's perfect other half.

Thus unfolds a battle of science against soul, perfection versus passion, that terrifies, twists, and turns . . . and meanwhile, the apocalypse is coming.

arrow books

We support

I'm proud to support the National Literacy Trust, an independent charity that changes lives through literacy.

Did you know that millions of people in the UK struggle to read and write? This means children are less likely to succeed at school and less likely to develop into confident and happy teenagers. Literacy difficulties will limit their opportunities throughout adult life.

The National Literacy Trust passionately believes that everyone has a right to the reading, writing, speaking and listening skills they need to fulfil their own and, ultimately, the nation's potential.

My own son didn't used to enjoy reading which was why I started writing children's books – reading for pleasure is an essential way to encourage children to pick up a book. The National Literacy Trust is dedicated to delivering exciting initiatives to encourage people to read and to help raise literacy levels. To find out more about the great work that they do visit their website at www.literacytrust.org.uk.

James Patterson